THE
LITTLE GIANT® BOOK

OF

"True" Ghostly Tales

THE
LITTLE GIANT® BOOK
OF
"True" Ghostly Tales

C. B. Colby, Ron Edwards, John Macklin,

Sharon McCoy, Sheryl Scarborough

Illustrated by Elise Chanowitz,
Dianne O'Quinn Burke, and Jim Sharpe

Sterling Publishing Co., Inc.
New York

Stories in this book were excerpted from:
World's Best True Ghost Stories by C.B. Colby, © 1990 by Sterling
Publishing Co., Inc.; *World's Best Lost Treasure Stories*, © 1991 by
C.B. Colby; *World's Strangest True Ghost Stories* by John Macklin, ©
1991 by Sterling Publishing Co., Inc.; *World's Most Mystifying True
Ghost Stories* © 1997 by Ron Edwards; *Scary Howl of Fame* by Sheryl
Scarborough and Sharon McCoy, © 1995 by RGA Publishing
Group, Inc.

10 9 8 7 6 5 4 3 2 1

© 2002 by Sterling Publishing Co., Inc.
387 Park Avenue South, New York, NY 10016
Distributed in Canada by Sterling Publishing
c/o Canadian Manda Group, One Atlantic Avenue, Suite 105
Toronto, Ontario, Canada M6K 3E7
Distributed in Great Britain by Chris Lloyd
at Orca Book Services,
Stanley House, Fleets Lane, Poole BH15 3AJ, England
Distributed in Australia by Capricorn Link (Australia) Pty. Ltd.
P.O. Box 704, Windsor, NSW 2756, Australia

Manufactured in China
All rights reserved

Sterling ISBN 1-4027-0369-4

CONTENTS

I. HAUNTED SOULS

Those who say they do not believe in ghosts have never read these stories. Haunted souls come back to earth for many dif-ferent reasons. Some visit those who know them. Others attempt to interact with strangers. Whatever the relationship, the ghosts in this chap-ter feel the need to express themselves to the living.

❧ Lavender ❧

In the fall of 1948, two students at the University of Chicago decided to escape the rigors of study in their stuffy dorm and attend a dance they had seen posted on the bulletin board. They had waited too long to find dates, but knew there would be many eager coeds at the festive affair.

While driving along the highway, they noticed a young girl slowly walking on the shoulder of the road. The boys stopped and invited the enchanting stranger to ride with them. She told them she was on her way to a dance and got into the car.

The boys introduced themselves and said they were also on their way to the dance. She smiled and said her name was the same as the lavender dress she was wearing. Although her beauty was alluring, there seemed to be something strange about their pretty passenger.

At the party, Lavender was an excellent dancer. All the boys surrendered to her beguiling charm and personality that evening. She captured the hearts of everyone except the other girls, who were virtually ignored by their dates.

When the dance hall closed, the two boys offered to take Lavender home. She smiled and slid onto the rear seat of the convertible. During the drive, the autumn air became chilly and one of the boys gave her his coat.

They were surprised when they arrived at her house. Lavender lived in a crumbling shack, standing precariously on a dirt road off the highway. They said good night and were soon on their way back to the campus.

During lunch the next day, the two students remembered that Lavender still had the coat. After class, they drove to the old shack on the outskirts of Chicago. They could not understand why such a wonderful girl had to live in such a grubby part of the city. An elderly woman answered their knock.

"Hello," said the older boy. "Is Lavender home?"

"Nobody named Lavender lives here," said the woman, who eyed the boys suspiciously. "What do you want?"

"She must live here," insisted the other boy. "We brought her home last night after a dance."

When he described her, the woman's face beamed with delight. "Oh, you must be talking about Lily. That's what she looked like. But Lily isn't here anymore." The old woman grinned shrewdly. "She lives in the cemetery down the road."

The two boys suddenly thought they were the victims of a practical joke and decided to let Lavender keep the jacket. She obviously did not own a coat or she would have worn it last night. Lavender could use some warm clothes if this hovel was really her home. They smiled, said good-bye to the old woman, and drove away in silence.

Out of curiosity, they went to the abandoned cemetery to check out the crazy story. Surely, the old woman was just having fun with them. As a matter of fact, she was probably still chuckling at their innocence.

At the cemetery, they began walking along the headstones and were mildly surprised to find a marker engraved with the name "Lily." But they were really shocked when they found their missing coat folded neatly on the grave.

✺ Joe Baldwin's Lantern ✺

During the 1800s, the nation's railroads were run by strong, dedicated men who were proud of their profession and heritage. Folk heroes such as Casey Jones and John Henry are known to everyone, but no one remembers Joe Baldwin. He was not an engineer or steel-driving man. Joe was a conductor for the Wilmington, Manchester, and Augusta Railway that operated through Georgia and the Carolinas.

One spring evening in 1868, he was aboard a freight train that was roaring through a raging storm to reach a siding and allow an express to pass.

Joe was sitting in the caboose when he suddenly felt the car slow down. He looked out the window and was astonished to see that the caboose had separated from the train.

The shrill whistle of the approaching express filled Joe Baldwin with terror. He saw its blinding

light racing toward him. He grabbed a red lantern, ran to the rear of the platform, and frantically waved a warning signal. He was still standing there when the express slammed into the caboose and exploded, covering the scene with a flaming shroud of wood and twisted steel.

Joe Baldwin's mangled body was found the next morning. His head was missing and never recovered. More than a century later, his headless spirit is still seen walking along the tracks west of Wilmington, waving a red lantern.

Skeptics will tell you the strange glow comes from automobile lights on Highway 87. The strange effect appears under certain atmospheric conditions when headlights are reflected off clouds to resemble a lantern. None of the experts, how-ever, can explain how the eerie image appeared during the 19th century, when cars didn't exist. Most railroad veterans are sure the persistent phantom is Joe Baldwin searching for his head.

❧ Message from the Dead ❧

A young mother lost her husband and became the sole parent of her four-year-old boy. Her future looked grim as she worried about paying the bills. She could not find her husband's insurance policy and would soon have to consider bankruptcy to escape impatient creditors. While she was working long hours in a hotel, her son spent most of his day playing in the lobby.

Two weeks after his father died, the boy began scribbling on a sheet of paper. He filled three pages with nonsensical doodles and put them in his mother's mailbox.

The morning desk clerk called her attention to the unusual characters, which somehow resembled shorthand. But neither the boy nor his mother understood that form of writing.

She gave the papers to the hotel stenographer, who managed to decipher the strange language.

The simple message mentioned a special name the child's father had used when referring to his wife. Then a startling fact was revealed: The family's important documents, bonds, and insurance policy could be found in a safe deposit box at a bank in New York City.

Later, the items were recovered and saved the young widow from financial ruin.

One odd note was that the woman's husband had once been a stenographer. The mother could not explain how her four-year-old boy received the lifesaving information, but accepted it as a message from the grave.

❧ Dead Man's Inn ❧

On September 30, 1980, a dilapidated inn burned to the ground in Tisakurt, Hungary. Although the fire was intentional, no one cared to find the unknown arsonist. The simmering timbers were all that remained of a haunted building that had been a haven of horror for sixty years.

One unfortunate guest described a spine-chilling sight while staying at the inn. The German tourist was frightened senseless one evening when he opened the dining room door. He saw a large table surrounded by ten rotting corpses, each holding a glass of wine. They were wearing ragged clothes from the Roaring '20s and their lips were curled back, revealing a hideous grin.

Then everyone at the table slowly turned to face him and raised their glasses in a toast to the dead. The terrified man ran away and never looked back.

The citizens of Tisakurt knew what had happened and were relieved to see the haunted house finally destroyed. Perhaps the evil inn's grisly legend had also perished in the smoldering ashes.

It all began in 1919 when Lazio Kronberg and

his wife, Susi, faced a bleak future after spending all their savings to keep the inn open.

Poverty was just another direful circumstance they would have to accept after suffering several other tragedies. Their youngest son and daughter had run away from home years ago, and two older boys had died during the recent war.

There was only one way to escape bankruptcy. The desperate innkeepers decided to pursue a new venture that would satisfy their creditors. Although apprehensive about resorting to crime for survival, they thought it was the only solution, and so, bought bags of quicklime and poison.

Lazio told curious guests the quicklime was going to be used for a new outhouse, while Susi explained that the strychnine would eliminate pesky rats.

Lazio filled a large trench with quicklime, but the offensive rodents never dined on strychnine soup. The poison was added to glasses of wine and served to the Kronbergs' guests during dinner. The victims' valuables were then removed before the bodies were tossed into the trench. Local authorities estimated that ten unfortunate customers enjoyed their last glass of wine at the inn before the summer of 1922.

The last candidate for the quicklime trench signed the inn's register on August 14, 1922.

"Just call me Lucky," said the jovial salesman in his thirties. "I've been very successful and now I'm searching for investment property. In fact, I'm thinking about settling here in Tisakurt."

After dinner, Lazio had an unusual feeling about Lucky and did not want to harm him. But Susi objected furiously. She had been eyeing the new guest's heavy suitcase and was sure it contained money or jewels.

They served Lucky the strychnine sherry and waited impatiently for him to collapse. Susi's suspicions proved true, and Lazio was thrilled to find the suitcase filled with gold. He also found a faded photograph at the bottom of the bag.

Lazio and Susi studied the photo and soon recognized it as a picture of the Kronberg family that was taken years ago.

The two innkeepers were horrified to discover they had just killed their long-lost son, Nicholas, who ran away when he was nine years old. He had become a prosperous salesman and told his friends he was going back home to surprise his parents with a gift of gold coins. He drank the fatal glass of wine before revealing his true identity.

Lazio and Susi were found in the same position as the grotesque diners who were seen by the German tourist. The murderous couple penned a complete confession before joining Nicholas at the table. They drank a glass of strychnine wine and were found by the villagers three days later.

The inn was operated by several owners before and after World War II. Each proprietor admitted seeing the ghosts of Lazio, Susi, and the murdered guests who ate their last meal at the sinister inn. The ghastly visions were still being seen where so many came to spend the night and never checked out.

Evidence in the
❧ Graveyard ❧

Eerie things are sighted in graveyards, but few of them remain in place for all the world to see. A heinous crime, which occurred in Washta, Iowa, in Cherokee County at the turn of the 20th century, was followed by one of the most ominous sights ever seen on a tombstone!

Heinrich and Olga Schultz, husband and wife, were a kind, elderly couple who lived on a small farm in Iowa. They were well liked and had no enemies. In fact, neighbors and townspeople all respected and admired the Schultzes because of their honest nature and willingness to help other people.

Therefore, it was a sickening shock that they were murdered in cold blood, in the middle of a frigid winter night. Their bodies were found in their home—their heads split open with an ax!

There were signs everywhere of a struggle. Heinrich and Olga had fought hard to save their lives, but unfortunately lost the battle. When the townspeople heard the news of their brutal deaths, they shivered with outrage … and fear.

Three days before his death, Heinrich had withdrawn his life savings from the bank, feeling it would be safer at home. When the bodies were

found, the money was gone—along with the Schultzes' hired hand and boarder, Will Florence. Everyone, including the authorities, was convinced that Will had murdered the couple and stolen the money. Will had always been a troublemaker, but Heinrich had felt the need to give him a chance by offering him work around the farm.

An aggressive manhunt ensued, and Will was finally found hiding out in Nebraska. The police couldn't get their hands on enough physical evidence to convict him · of the murders, so he was released.

In the weeks to come, a strange phenomenon began to unfold at the graveyard where the Schultzes were buried. A face began to appear in the marble of the joint headstone that the couple shared. Over the course of three or four weeks, the picture grew clearer and clearer. Just as film under chemical action develops a negative, the marble tombstone developed the picture of a face. Rumor of this event circulated, and eventually, law enforcement officials visited the graveyard. Even the most skeptical detectives gasped in shock when they saw it. The perfect likeness of Will was etched into the tombstone.

Several months later, new evidence implicating Will Florence as the murderer surfaced, but although an enormous search took place, he was never found. To this day, however, his guilt remains stamped upon the marble tombstone atop the Schultzes' grave, which still stands in Cherokee County.

II. GHOST IN THE HOUSE

Why is a house haunted? Why does a ghost need to remain in it, endlessly repeating the same actions? The hauntings in this chapter are of vastly different types, but every one of them reveals the obsession of a troubled spirit.

❧ House for Sale ❧

"Drive a little slower, dear," Therese Storrer said to her husband. "There's a house for sale."

Hans-Peter Storrer stepped on the brake, and the car slowed down, its spoked wheels brushing the roadside grass.

It was July 1908, and Therese and Hans-Peter Storrer were on the threshold of the strangest and most unaccountable experience of their lives. They were about to negotiate for a home of their own—with a family of ghosts.

The story of the Storrers, which unfolded in a village in the hills outside Vienna, has become a classic of Austrian psychic research. "Of all my investigations, this is the only case for which I can offer absolutely no rational explanation," wrote Dr. Paul Bonvin, a famous investigator of supernatural phenomena who died in 1925.

As the car coasted to a halt, Hans-Peter, a twenty-eight-year-old bank official, pushed up his

dark glasses and examined the dusty "For Sale" notice.

The couple had been married for two years and had spent all that time living in the cramped flat of Therese's parents. They were searching anxiously for a house of their own, preferably in the country but reasonably near Vienna.

Hans-Peter swung the car around and started slowly up the narrow lane toward a house standing high above them on green sloping ground. As he drove, he noticed how grassed-over and lacking in recent wheel marks the lane was.

The observation meant little to him at the moment. Later it slipped starkly, logically into place. For dead men don't drive cars.

A few minutes later, they reached a set of open iron gates leading onto a weedy courtyard. The house, in pale flaking brick, stood across an over-grown lawn. It was neglected; its paint was peeling. But there was no doubt that it had once been an elegant house.

Hans-Peter stopped the car and helped his wife out. They waited a few moments, but no one came to the door; no faces appeared at the window.

There was a curious oppressive silence, broken only by the couple's footsteps as they walked toward the front door.

Later, Therese recalled what happened next: "We stood at the door, and Hans-Peter knocked. We heard the knocks resounding through the house—an eerie sound—but no one answered. There were curtains at the windows, and there appeared to be furniture inside. We were quite sure the house was inhabited.

"Eventually, my husband tried the door. It was unlocked. There seemed little harm in having a quick look around now that we had gone this far. He went in first and I followed."

The house was dim and filled with cobwebs. The furnishings that filled every room were thick with dust, riddled with the ravages of moth and worm. In the kitchen, crockery and cutlery were laid out on a table for a meal that obviously had never been served. In the pantry, bread and vegetables, laid on the marble slabs, had long since rotted away.

All the trappings of living were there in the decaying, neglected house. Only the people were missing.

Therese continued the story: "By this time I was ready to leave—I wouldn't have lived there however reasonable the price. But Hans-Peter was determined to look over the rest of the place.

"We walked along a gloomy corridor and opened a door to what I assumed to be the main living room of the house. The door swung back and we both saw them clearly. There *were* people in the house.

"Heavy curtains hung at the windows, but there was still enough light for me to be certain of what I saw. There were four people in the room—a man, a woman, and two children. They were sitting motionless in chairs around the fireplace. It was like a weird tableau.

"After what seemed like hours—it could only have been seconds—they turned and looked at us. They were wearing clothes in vogue in the 1890s and the man held a silver-topped cane.

"Strangely, my first reaction was not one of fear or horror. I just thought how pale and sad they all looked …"

Slowly, the image faded before the visitors' eyes and finally vanished completely. Not surprisingly, the Storrers wasted no time in putting as many miles as possible between themselves and the house on the hill!

It couldn't have been a hallucination, because they had both witnessed it. Afterward they separately recounted what they had seen, and the details tallied exactly.

It was over six months before Hans-Peter Storrer could bring himself to drive back to the village in the hills to seek an answer to the mystery that had been plaguing him. And he found it at the first place he visited—the tiny post office run by Ludwig Wahlen.

"That house, sir, has been for sale for nearly ten years," Herr Wahlen said. "There was a shooting tragedy up there. The master shot his wife and two children. It was in all the papers."

He rummaged in a drawer and produced a yellowed sheet of newsprint. A large photograph headed the page. Looking at it, Hans-Peter saw again the sad, pale faces of the dead family he had witnessed in the house on the hill.

The Thing in
❧ the Cellar ❦

This ghost tale from New Jersey may illustrate the moral that if you happen to have a ghost in your house, the most practical course of action is to be hospitable. It might even pay off in hard cash ...

It seems that a house in Trenton had been known to be haunted for many years, and

nobody would rent it, in spite of its being an attractive little cottage in a nice neighborhood. Finally a local man with a rather bad reputation appeared and offered to take it over. The owner informed him of the house's reputation and detailed its history. The man was not at all fazed. He laughed and signed the lease, saying he wasn't afraid of man, monster, or ghost.

One night, after living in the house about a week, the tenant had to go into the cellar. He took a candle and headed down. He was two steps above its stone floor when a huge black "thing" rose up at the bottom of the stairs. It had two glowing yellow-white eyes that seemed to stare clear through him. The man was startled but instead of fleeing he swore at the phantom and hurled his candlestick at it.

The neighbors found him a day or so later. He was alive, but all his hair was burned off, and he was a mass of bruises from head to toe. He moved out as soon as he was able to.

The next tenant was a gentle elderly lady who did a great deal of work for the local church. She had heard about the phantom, but the little house was inexpensive and it suited her, and she decided to move in, ghost or no ghost. She would take her chances, she said. It was lucky for her that she did.

After several days in the house with no disturbance, she too had to go to the cellar after dark. As the gleam of the candle lit up the stone cellar, the gruesome thing rose up before her. She held the candle higher and said very calmly, "My, you startled me, my friend, but what in the name of heaven do you want? Is there anything I can do to help you, as long as we are going to live here together?"

To her astonishment the black shape motioned for the lady to follow. It slowly drifted back across the stone flagging of the floor to an old wooden chest in the corner. She followed with the candle and obeyed the directions of the "thing" when it motioned for her to move the chest aside. It was empty, and she moved it easily. She found a loose flagstone underneath. The murky figure motioned for her to lift the flagstone, and again, she complied.

Underneath it was a lead-lined box full of old

gold coins. She stared at them for a moment. Then, half to herself, she said, "Can these be for me?" and turned to look at the phantom. It was gone, but a cool breeze touched her on the cheek in an almost friendly caress.

❧ Baby Ghost ❧

Tales about baby ghosts are few to begin with, and seldom are they as tragic as this one from upstate New York.

Near the town of Sodus, which is just south of Lake Ontario and about halfway between Rochester and Oswego, there lived a widow and her one-year-old daughter. The recent death of her husband had left the woman somewhat demented. She was extremely nervous and afraid of thunderstorms and lightning.

One night a terrific storm came up from over the lake. The thunder and lightning banged and crashed about her small house for hours. As the storm's fury increased, the poor woman became increasingly panicky. Her baby in its small crib by the fireplace cried louder and louder. Finally the widow's nerves cracked completely and she went mad.

No one knows just what happened, but after the storm was over, a neighbor, who dropped by to see if she was all right, found the woman groveling on the floor of the little house. The baby was dead in its crib. After examining the small body, the neighbors decided that in a moment of insane rage, the poor woman had killed the child to stop its crying. The mother died a short time afterward, but for weeks whenever a thunderstorm came up, folks who passed the house claimed they could hear a baby crying inside, although they knew no one was there.

Some months later lightning struck the house and burned it flat. Only a ruin was left. Still, during thunderstorms, people continued to hear the baby crying above the wind and rain.

Finally, unnerved neighbors banded together to try to stop the cries by completely demolishing the chimney and fireplace. The stones of the chimney were spread about the countryside and all signs of the house were either filled in, covered up, or removed entirely from the site. Then and only then were the plaintive cries of the small child stilled so that folks could walk past the place where the house had been without hearing them.

They say, however, that even today, if the skies are black with an oncoming thunderstorm and lightning crackles across the hills far away, you may still hear a soft and low whimper from the clearing where the house once stood.

❋ The Headless Lady ❋

Charles Needham, recovering from an illness, rented a small cottage on the edge of the charming town of Canewdon in Southeast Essex, England. The year was 1895 and Needham was settling down to convalesce. The housekeeper he hired for day work seemed concerned that he

was planning to sleep in the cottage alone. She kept asking if he thought he would be "all right." He assured her that as far as he knew, he would be, and for two or three nights he was. Then something happened.

He was sitting and reading in the kitchen one midnight, when he was startled by a click of the door latch behind him. The door led to a backyard garden. He watched the latch lift and then slowly fall again. The door was securely bolted at top and bottom, and whoever it was outside did not try to push against it. Needham remembered that the front door was unbolted and hurried into the other room. As he slid the bolt home, the latch of that door too began to rise to the top of the slot. It hesitated a moment and then slowly dropped back into place.

Needham was sick with tuberculosis and not a fit match for an intruder. Nevertheless, he slid back the bolt and threw open the door. There was no one there. For several nights this continued, much to Needham's discomfort, but he decided not to mention the matter either to his housekeeper or to any of the townspeople. He was a lawyer from London and suspected that youngsters in the neighborhood might be having a little cruel fun with him. He would withstand their pranks, he decided. But a few weeks later he had to change his mind …

He had been visiting a friend in town, a chess-playing doctor, and his host had offered to drive him back to the cottage in his pony cart. They were jogging up to the entrance of the little lane leading to the cottage when suddenly the pony stopped and refused to go farther, in spite of blows from the whip. Needham explained it was only a short walk anyway and got out, thanking his friend for the lift.

As he hurried home, he saw a small light ahead of him along one side of the moonlit road. The trees were thick in that section. Needham assumed the light was a lantern held by another pedestrian on the way home, so he quickened his step to catch up.

A few yards farther on, the figure ahead stepped out into the moonlight, close by his cottage, stood a few moments, and then turned toward him. Needham turned and fled in terror.

The figure was a woman, but a woman without a head! Needham ran all the way to the "Chequers," a small inn down the road.

He gave a babbled description of what he had seen, and was amazed to learn that the headless lady was a well-known Canewdon resident who had been murdered and decapitated by her husband many years before. She had once lived in the cottage he had rented. Perhaps she had been trying to enter and set up housekeeping again when she found the doors bolted against her.

Needham slept at the inn that night. The next day, he moved.

Revenge of the
✵ Waterford Ghost ✵

It's not often that a ghost has a chance to get revenge on people who are still alive, but near Waterford, New York, one supposedly did just that.

Around the year 1900, there lived a carpenter, near the end of a barge canal. He was poor and sick with tuberculosis, but he still worked hard to support his wife and two children with earnings from odd jobs about the village.

Unfortunately, his own parents were particularly selfish, cruel, and mercenary. They demanded that he will them his house and property, which in case of his death would have gone to his wife. This, of course, the carpenter refused to do. Shortly before he died, however, he warned his parents that if they did anything to harm his family after he was gone, he would come back and haunt them as long as they lived. He would see to it, he said, that they would never make any profit from his house even if they did get it away from his wife.

As soon as their son had passed away, the parents undertook legal proceedings and managed to obtain possession of the property, evicting the impoverished wife and youngsters. The house was run-down, but usable, and they hoped to rent it rather quickly. So they closed the blinds and waited for a tenant. But no tenant ever rented it, for presently strange things began to happen.

Some of the neighbors, passing the empty house late at night, noticed lights shining between the shuttered windows and from between loose boards along the sides. At first they thought that perhaps the wife had come back and was living there secretly. They had liked the wife, so they did not investigate too carefully.

However, the lights started to wave about and flicker from within, far too mysteriously for comfort, and people began to cross the road when they passed that way after dark. Rumor spread that the son was making good his promise to keep his parents from making any money from the cottage. As no one wanted to rent the place, it fell more and more into disrepair. Even in its last years, when it was completely uninhabitable, the mysterious lights could still be seen.

The greedy parents nevertheless kept trying to rent or sell the place. No one would listen to them. The lights continued showing right up until the day when, with a muffled crash and a cloud of dry dust, the sagging roof fell in and the tottering walls collapsed into the cellar hole. Only then did the lights vanish, never to return.

No one could explain the mysterious lights, but many neighbors felt sure that the Waterford Ghost had gotten its revenge.

❋ The Ghost of Greylock ❋

I can vouch for this ghost-sighting personally. It happened to me.

I once hunted fairly regularly in Massachusetts with a friend named Dick Davis. On one trip, Davis and I decided to work our way up the slopes of Mt. Greylock, in the northwestern corner of the state between Adams and North

Adams. Mt. Greylock isn't huge (3,506 feet), but it is rugged, and there were plenty of white-tailed deer browsing on its slopes.

We slept the first night in a haymow and went off separately the next morning. We planned to meet late in the afternoon at a deserted farmhouse we saw upon the slope.

About midafternoon I was hunting along the edge of a swamp when I was startled to hear the shrill blast of a police whistle through the brush. I knew I hadn't passed any red lights, so I waited to see what was coming. It turned out to be an old fellow who lived in the area and was hunting rabbits with an eager beagle. The whistle was to call the pup. We got to talking and I mentioned my plan to meet Davis at the old farmhouse later. The hunter looked at me sharply.

"Wouldn't go there, son!" he said. "Better meet your friend out in front."

When I asked him why I shouldn't go into the old house, he mumbled something about "bad flooring," then picked up his shotgun and left with the pup at his heels.

When I got to the farmhouse later, however, I did go in and decided to wait in one of the upstairs rooms. It overlooked an orchard where a few apples might still attract a deer. I settled down to wait. The floors and stairs seemed firm enough to me, even if the old building was run-down, long deserted, and had a corner of its roof missing.

About a half-hour after I'd arrived, I heard Dick climb the porch steps, knock snow and mud from his boots, and come in. I decided to keep still and give him a bit of a scare should he start up the stairs. I heard him walking around down below, opening and shutting the old cupboard doors. Then he came to the foot of the stairs just below the room in which I was squatting by the window. He started up and I expected to see his red knitted cap appear over the top step any second. It didn't appear. Perhaps he had seen my muddy tracks and decided to surprise me, I thought. He was waiting on the stairs. Okay, I'd outwait him.

A half-hour later I still was crouching by the window, waiting. I hadn't heard another sound from the person on the stairs, and by now I was in a rather nervous state, even if I did have a loaded shotgun in my hands. Suddenly a movement in the orchard below caught my eye. It was DICK!

Gun ready, I rose and crept out of the room. The stairs were deserted. I rushed out of the house to meet Dick and never went back in. I've often wondered who or what had started up those old stairs to where I waited, and then changed its mind, for as I hurried out of the house I noticed there were no other tracks but mine on the faded yellow floor.

III. JINXED!

In and of themselves, inanimate objects cannot be evil, carry curses, or warn of disasters and death. Can they? But what if they do? These next accounts illustrate the idea of personification in the scariest of ways.

The Spell on
⇒ the Mirror ⇐

In the War Memorial Hospital at Sault Ste. Marie, Michigan, Jefferey Derosier was close to death. He knew he was critically ill, and so did the three other patients who shared the small ward.

One afternoon Derosier asked the nurse to hand him the small mirror from the enamel table beside his bed. The nurse gave him the

mirror, which was just a plain piece of silvered glass without a frame or handle.

A moment later he threw it back upon the bedside table and cried hysterically, "I'm dying!" The other patients, watching him, were stunned. He spoke again in a low, dull voice. "You won't be able to pick up that mirror," he said. Then he died.

After his body had been removed, one of the other patients casually tried to pick up the mirror. He couldn't budge it from where it lay on the white table. Baffled, he asked the nurse to pick it up, but she couldn't move it either.

A doctor was called, and he too tried to lift the mirror from its place. It would not move. Soon word of the "haunted" mirror spread throughout the hospital. Nurses, interns, and curious patients all tried to move the little mirror from where the dying man had thrown it. No one succeeded. All day the mirror defied every attempt to move it. Even when a nurse tried to pry it loose with an ice pick, it remained sealed to the tabletop.

Then another nurse tried to work her fingernail under the edge of the little piece of glass. As if at that moment the spell was broken, the mirror flew several feet into the air and fell to the floor unbroken. At last it had moved.

Trying to find a reason for the mirror sticking to the table as long as it had, some of the witnesses attempted to make it stick again. But they couldn't do it. There was no adhesive on the back of the piece of silvered glass and anyone could now pick it up easily from the dry tabletop. They wet the surface in an attempt to create suction so that the mirror would stick once more, but the spell was broken.

Later the mirror was cracked, perhaps on purpose, and thrown away. There was never any explanation of the spell cast by Jefferey Derosier's dying words.

A Car with Murder
❧ in Its Heart ❧

The dark-green open touring car with bright emerald upholstery rolled out of its garage into the June sunshine, and Count Franz Harrach contemplated it with an anxious frown.

It was the newest, most expensive car in the city of Sarajevo and was to be used that day to take the Archduke Franz Ferdinand, heir to the throne of Austria, on a tour of welcome through the city.

And yet, the car, a 1912 Graf and Sift, had a reputation. It was the central figure in a series of bizarre accidents. Disaster struck many of those who came in contact with it.

In the summer of 1913, Count Harrach's chauffeur mowed down two peasants in a lane outside Sarajevo, killing both of them and seriously injuring himself.

Six months later, the car was involved in another accident in which a young nobleman lost his right arm. Was it coincidence? Eventually, the Count convinced himself that it was. He permitted the Archduke to ride in the Graf and Sift through the streets of Sarajevo—and fall victim to a murderer's bullet, in an assassination that was to plunge the world into war.

It was on Sunday, June 28, 1914, that the Archduke and his wife entered Sarajevo. The sun was shining, the crowd was friendly. The threat of violence seemed remote indeed.

The Graf and Sift was second in the motorcade. The Archduke sat in the left rear seat with his wife beside him. Next to them, on folding seats, sat the Governor of Bosnia and Count Harrach.

As the procession approached the City Council Chamber, a young anarchist named Nedjelko Cabrinovik threw a homemade bomb into the royal car. The bomb landed on the rolled-up hood.

Instantly, Archduke Ferdinand wheeled around and swept the device into the road. The car lurched forward as the driver jammed down the accelerator.

But the jinxed car was not yet finished with the Archduke.

Five minutes later, another assassin, Vagrilo Princip, pushed his way through the crowd, raised a pistol, and shot Ferdinand through the throat. A second shot burst through the side of the car and seriously wounded the Archduchess.

They were two of the most fateful shots in history. A month later, Austria declared war on Serbia. Russia came to the aid of Serbia, Germany sided with Austria, and within six weeks of the murder, the whole of Europe was at war.

Count Harrach became an officer in the Serbian Army and used the Graf and Sift as his staff car. Three officers carried in it were killed in an ambush. The car spent the rest of the war in a farmyard.

Afterward, it carried on a war of its own. It was sold to a Serbian government official who, one day in 1919, collided with a train at a level crossing. The official was thrown out and killed. The car was undamaged.

The driver's relatives ordered the jinxed car to be demolished, but a doctor asked to be allowed to buy it. He was crushed to death when it overturned.

A Swiss racing driver became the next ill-fated owner. He had it completely rebuilt and modified, and entered it in a French Automobile Club race in Orleans. In third place, the car suddenly veered off the road and came to rest in a ditch. As usual, it was undamaged, but the driver was dead. A medical examination revealed that he had died of a heart attack.

A farmer near Paris became the next owner and used the car without incident for nearly two years. One morning, he was about to leave for the market when the vehicle stalled and refused to restart. It roared into life after a tow from a tractor.

As the farmer walked around to the front of the vehicle, it unaccountably slipped into gear, jerked forward, and ran its owner down.

Once again it was sold. Once again it was bought by a man who scoffed at the idea of a car being jinxed. The new owner had the bodywork modified and the color changed to black. But the car still had murder in its heart.

It claimed five more victims—four passengers and the new owner—before it was locked in a garage in Strasbourg. So lurid was its reputation that no wrecker would attempt to dismantle it.

The job was finally done by Allied bombers in World War II, and the curse of the Graf and Sift was broken at last.

❊ Valentino's Ring ❊

In the vault of a Los Angeles bank lies a silver ring set with a semiprecious stone. It is not a particularly pretty ring or even a very valuable one, and chances are that no one will ever dare to wear it again. It lies in the vault because it bears one of the most malignant curses in the history of the occult. Successive owners have suffered injury, misfortune, even death.

And many people still believe it was this ring that sent Rudolph Valentino to a premature grave.

Certainly, the violent incidents that have surrounded it over the years can hardly be shrugged off as mere coincidences.

It was in 1920 that Valentino, at the peak of his success, saw the ring in a San Francisco jeweller's. The proprietor warned him that the ring was a jinx, but Valentino still bought it.

He wore the ring in his next picture, *The Young Rajah.* It was the biggest flop of his career and he was off the screen for the next two years.

Valentino did not wear the ring again until he used it as a costume prop in *The Son of the Sheik.* Three weeks after finishing this film, he went to New York on vacation.

While wearing the ring, he suffered an acute attack of appendicitis. Two weeks later, he was dead.

Pola Negri, a famous female movie star of the time, asked to pick a memento from Valentino's possessions, chose the ring—and almost immediately suffered a long period of ill health that threatened to end her career.

A year later, while convalescing, she met a performer who was almost Valentino's double, Russ Colombo. Miss Negri was so struck by the resemblance that she gave him Rudolph's ring, saying, "From one Valentino to another."

Within a few days of receiving the gift, Russ Colombo was killed in a freak shooting accident.

His cousin passed the ring on to Russ's best friend, Joe Casino. Also at the height of his popularity as an entertainer, Casino took no chances with the ring. Instead of wearing it, he kept it in a glass case in memory of his dead friend. When he was asked to donate it to a museum of Valentino relics, he refused, saying that he treasured it for sentimental reasons.

As time passed, Joe Casino forgot the ring's evil reputation and put it on. A week later, still wearing the ring, he was knocked down by a truck and killed.

By now the curse was front-page news. When asked what he proposed to do with the ring, Joe's brother, Del, explained that he could not allow himself to be intimidated by a curse, or jinx, or ghost, or whatever it was. He didn't believe in things like that.

Del Casino wore the ring for some time and nothing unusual happened. Then he lent it to a collector of Valentino relics, who suffered no ill effects either. This caused several newspapers to speculate that at last the evil influence of the ring had come to an end. And that seemed to trigger off a new wave of violence.

One night soon afterward, the home of Del Casino was burgled. The police saw the burglar, a man named James Willis, running from the scene. One of them fired a warning shot, but the bullet went low and killed Willis. Among the loot found in his possession was the Valentino ring.

It was at this time that Hollywood producer Edward Small decided to make a film based on Valentino's career.

Jack Dunn, a former skating partner to ice star Sonja Henie, bore a great resemblance to Rudolph and was asked to make a film test for the part. He dressed in Valentino's clothes for the test—and also wore the jinxed ring.

Only twenty-one years old at the time, Dunn died ten days later from a rare blood disease.

After this tragedy the ring was kept out of sight and never worn by anyone again, but that did not seem to curb its fatal influence.

A year after Jack Dunn's death, a daring raid was carried out in broad daylight on a Los Angeles bank in which thieves got away with a haul of over $200,000. In a subsequent police ambush, two of the gang were caught and three passers-by seriously injured. The leader of the bank robbers, Alfred Hahn, was jailed for life.

At his trial, Hahn remarked: "If I'd known what was in the vault apart from money, I'd have picked myself another bank."

For in the bank's safe deposit vault was the Valentino ring.

Can an inanimate object exert a malign influence on those who come into contact with it? All those who have suffered the jinx of Valentino's ring have little doubt that it can. And who can blame them?

☆ Ghost Truck ☆

Just before twelve o'clock on a February night in 1930, a group of men gathered by the side of a lonely lane in northwest England. The men were members of a coroner's jury. They had come out to this desolate spot—to seek out a ghost.

Earlier in the month, two men on a motorcycle had crashed in very mysterious circumstances on this same road. The driver died, but his passenger lived to tell the tale.

At the inquest, the passenger insisted that they had had to swerve violently on the night in question because a truck had suddenly backed out of an opening right across their path.

Yet police had inspected the stretch of road—and found there was no opening of any kind in the area from which a truck could have emerged.

"But I saw it as plain as can be!" burst in the passenger at the inquest.

"It was probably some form of optical illusion," the coroner commented, but the passenger wouldn't accept the idea.

"There is an opening there. I'll show it to you," he insisted.

"In view of the great number of accidents that have taken place on that particular stretch of road during the past twenty-two months, I think it would be as well if this jury were to examine the scene of the mishap," the coroner declared. "So far, no satisfactory explanation for any of these accidents has been forthcoming, and I think it is time the mystery was solved."

Because every one of the accidents had taken place at night, the coroner added that it might be best if they visited the spot at "the witching hour."

"If there really is a phantom truck, then it should, according to ghost lore, appear at midnight," he concluded with a smile.

Altogether, three people had been killed and an additional twenty-five injured at the spot in question. Eighteen cars had been involved in crashes, most of the drivers swearing that a vehicle of some sort had suddenly materialized across their path, seemingly from thin air.

Local residents were firmly convinced that a phantom vehicle was to blame. There were ghost ships, phantom armies, and haunted coaches—why not a ghost truck?

"There are ghosts in these parts," they told the reporters. "You can hear them marching up and down the street at night. But when you go to look out of the window, there's nobody there.

"What's more, you can't get a dog to walk along that stretch of road at night. They can see something that sets them howling in terror."

The owner of a pub in the neighborhood went further and declared that every time the ghost walked, an accident took place. "There's no mistaking the tread," he told newspapermen. "It sounds like a very big man clumping along. I've heard it in the courtyard quite often—always late at night and at the full moon. And then, without fail, somebody is found the next morning either dead or dying on the road."

And so, at midnight, February 18, 1930, the motorcycle passenger led the jury to the scene of the accident. Try though he might, however, he could not discover an opening of any sort.

"I can't understand it," he muttered, completely bewildered. "We both saw it backing out of this lane, or whatever it was."

"It was probably a patch of mist," remarked one of the jury members.

"This hedge and the wall adjoining caught in the sudden glare of a headlight could very well be mistaken for the back of a truck," ventured another.

The ghost truck did not put in an appearance that night, but soon afterward a huge trailer truck went off the road at the exact same spot.

A few nights after that, a motorcyclist thought he saw something blocking the road ahead. He braked sharply and went careening into the hedge.

And so it went. A member of the Society for Psychical Research spent an entire night by the side of the road, but the phantom eluded him.

Police were convinced that the wall and the hedge were to blame and had them removed in due course. The accidents became less frequent, but they do still occasionally happen.

And it still takes a brave—or unimaginative—person to walk down that lonely lane at midnight when the moon is high …

The Man and
❧ the Glove ❧

While sight-seeing in Scotland, a young American woman joined a group that was visiting an island where a crumbling castle had recently been opened to the public. As they approached the castle, the young lady noticed that a huge cloud overhead looked like a pair of gauntlet gloves. She called it to the attention of the others

in the party, but thought no more about it. The unusual cloud formation soon faded away.

Later that day a sudden and violent storm came up. Because the trip back to the mainland was too rough for their small boat, the sight-seers were forced to spend the night at the castle. The young American was given a room in one of the towers. She went to bed quite thrilled at the opportunity to spend the night there.

Awakening during the night, she was surprised to see a pair of white gauntlets on the floor by her bed. The gloves were surrounded by a halo of light that illuminated a crest embroidered in red silk. As the bewildered woman raised her eyes from the strange sight, she was even more startled to see a tall, dark young man looking at her from the shadows beyond the gloves. At her gasp of terror, both the glowing gloves and the young man vanished.

Perhaps, she thought, it had been a dream, inspired by the gauntlet-shaped cloud she had seen earlier. She didn't mention her ghostly visitor to anyone.

Several years passed. In New York, she met a young Scotsman and married him. Shortly after their honeymoon, he received word that a maiden aunt had died in New England, and the newlyweds had to go there to close the house. It was very run-down and dilapidated, with hardly a

sign that it had been lived in. The young bride occupied herself by poking about the attic. There in an old trunk, neatly wrapped in a bit of tartan, was a pair of white gauntlets, exactly the same as those she had seen in the castle years before.

She hurried downstairs in excitement to show them to her husband and tell him about the strange coincidence. When she held them out to him, he turned deathly pale. "So, my dear," he said, "you were the girl in the bed that night!" Then he vanished—for the second time! His bride fainted, and when she came to, she was alone. Questioning the neighbors later, she was told that no one had lived in the old house for a hundred years. She never saw her husband again.

IV. OFF THE TIME TRACK?

Probably all of us, at one time or other, have encountered something that seemed out of sync. It might be a vision of something that didn't belong—perhaps something in the wrong place at the wrong time. Here are a few curious tales of events that may have been off the time track.

⤜ **Mystery at the Palace** ⤛

When people talk about time travel, one story is quoted more than any other. It is, perhaps, the most astonishing and well documented ghost story of all.

It was on a summer's day in 1901 that two women visitors to France's Palace of Versailles traveled back two hundred years in time—to the spacious, leisurely days of the 18th century.

They saw buildings that had been demolished generations before, watched people strolling about in clothes they had previously seen only in museums—and saw Marie Antoinette sketching on the lawn!

There is no rational explanation for the strange experiences encountered by Anne Moberly, principal of St. Hugh's College, Oxford, and her friend Eleanor Jourdain, the college's lecturer in French, during a vacation they spent together in France.

While visiting the Palace of Versailles near the end of their trip, they went looking for the Petit Trianon, Marie Antoinette's summer home. Having only a small guidebook map, they didn't notice the deserted drive that would have led to their destination, and they got lost.

Following a narrow lane, they found themselves walking through thickly wooded glades that led to a group of farm buildings.

Accounts that both women later compiled

showed that at the time both of them noticed an eerie stillness in the air.

They asked their way of two men, dressed in long, greyish-green coats. Because of a wheel barrow and a spade nearby, the women assumed that the men were gardeners. "We did not realize at the time," wrote Miss Jourdain later, "that the style of their dress was at least two hundred years old."

Miss Jourdain noticed a woman and a girl standing at the stone steps of a cottage. That was to prove a most significant detail.

Even a little later, when the women met a man wearing a wide-brimmed hat and cloak that would only have been worn at a fancy dress ball, the incident still did not strike them as odd!

This man had a pockmarked face and an extremely dark complexion. Both women felt frightened by him. They were greatly relieved when another man ran up to them crying: "May I show you the way, mesdames?"

He indicated a small bridge over a ravine. Presently, they arrived at a clearing in front of the Petit Trianon. On a stool, a woman sat sketching.

Once again, the teachers noticed that curious air of oppressiveness. And, once again, it seemed that some alien agent had willed them to disregard the fact that everyone they saw was dressed almost two hundred years behind the times.

It was only after the two women returned to Paris that they began comparing notes. Then they realized they had each seen things the other hadn't.

Miss Moberly said it was a pity they hadn't spoken to the woman who was sketching, only for her friend to deny having seen such a woman.

Similarly, Miss Moberly had not witnessed the woman and the girl seen by her friend.

Three months later, Miss Jourdain made a second trip to the Petit Trianon. The joyful sound of music drifted across the park and she noted the tune that was being played. She also saw two laborers in red-and-blue capes filling a cart with sticks.

She was shattered when the caretaker of the Petit Trianon told her that no band had played that day and also laughed at her story of having seen men in red-and-blue capes. "Such capes haven't been worn for two hundred years," he told the astonished woman.

A few weeks later, both teachers made another pilgrimage to Versailles together. Many of the landmarks they had both seen the first time were gone.

It became clear to them, that in some strange, inexplicable way, they had been given a glimpse of Versailles as it was in Marie Antoinette's day.

In the archives of the French Academy of History, Miss Moberly found some proof to support this incredible theory. The grey-green costume they had seen proved to have been the old royal livery. Two brothers in this garb had always been on duty near the cottage when the Queen was in residence.

The cottage Miss Jourdain had noticed where the woman and a girl stood was identified on an old engraving. Records showed that in 1789, a fourteen-year-old girl and her mother had lived there.

A kiosk that both had seen was found on a map of 1783. And at that time, the Queen's intimate friends had included a Comte de

Vaudreuil—a pockmarked Creole, who often wore a large cloak and a Spanish hat.

The music Miss Jourdain heard proved to have been a tune of the period around 1780.

The two friends inspected pictures of Marie Antoinette. One of them was very much like the sketching woman that Miss Moberly had seen.

They could not trace the bridge and ravine they had crossed until an old map was found stuffed up a chimney. Drawn in the hand of Marie Antoinette's landscape gardener, it clearly showed the bridge and ravine.

Many people now believe that in some mysterious way, the women had been transported into the past—but why?

"I would not have believed such a thing could happen, had I read it or been told of it," Miss Moberly wrote, "but now I know that indeed all things are possible."

The Phantom
❧ Stagecoach ❧

Many years ago there was a small Arizona frontier town that was kept alive by a nearby gold mine. The town had once been on the stagecoach route, but when the mine petered out and was abandoned, the stage line was discontinued. Now the little town was almost completely cut off from

the rest of the settlements. Only a tiny freight line, run infrequently by a local livery stable owner, remained.

One young boy in the poverty-stricken town was always exploring the nearby hills, hoping to find another mine to bring back the people who had moved away, and also the stagecoach, which he had loved. He had always been there to meet the stage-coach when it came tearing into the little town in a cloud of dust.

The other people in town looked upon the boy's prospecting with amusement, but they did not bother him. In fact, they hoped that he would find a mine and bring prosperity back to the town.

One day the boy left for the hills as usual, with his burro and his lunch, but by nightfall he had not returned. As he had always been back by dark before, his folks became concerned. True, he was self-reliant and used to the rough living of the times and the area, but anything might have happened.

Finally, just after midnight, he came home, exhausted but excited. The stagecoach, he said, had come back to town after all.

Then he told this story. He had become separated from his burro back in the hills, and after searching for a long time, he gave up and started home on foot. It was dark by the time he reached the old coach road to town, and he could hear the howls of wolves in the timber of the foothills close by.

He hurried, but the cries of the wolves behind him became louder and louder. In panic he climbed to the top of a high rock by the roadside to wait for the pack to close in.

Just as the wolves approached, he heard the noise of a stagecoach coming along the old road. A huge stagecoach drawn by black, shining horses pulled around the bend and came to a leather-creaking stop beside the rock where the boy clung in terror. The driver motioned for him to climb in, and the coach raced toward town with the wolves howling right behind.

His parents had trouble believing the boy's story. No one had seen the stagecoach in years, and the boy was known to have an active imagination. But the strangest part was to come to light the next day.

Just outside of town, a huge grey wolf was found, obviously run over by a heavy wagon or stagecoach. The tracks of the vehicle came right to the edge of town, and then they stopped. They did not turn around and go back—they just stopped, as though they had vanished with the coach that made them.

Something had brought the boy back to safety—and it was certainly more substantial than imagination.

Hitchhiker to
❯❯ Montgomery ❮❮

Driving toward Montgomery, Alabama, late one evening, two businessmen planned to spend the night in a small town along the way. They were making good time through some low country when their headlights picked up a figure far ahead. As they drew nearer, they discovered that it was a tiny, elderly lady walking briskly along the side of the road. Slowing down to speak to her, they saw that she wore a pale sky-blue dress, freshly pressed and sparkling clean. Her hair was neatly done and she turned a smiling face to

them. She seemed completely untroubled about walking down a lonely highway in the middle of the night.

When the men asked what she was doing on the road at that time of night, she laughingly explained that she had started out to visit her daughter and grandchildren in Montgomery. She had hoped, she said, to get a ride for at least part of the way, but no one had offered her a lift, so she had just kept on walking.

The two men said they would give her a ride as far as the next town, a two-hour drive, and she was delighted to accept. She sat in the back seat and, as they drove through the night, talked about her daughter and three grandchildren— their names, where they lived, the children's school—the usual small talk among strangers. When the subject was exhausted, the men became engrossed in business conversation and forgot about the passenger behind them.

When they reached their destination, they stopped to let the elderly woman out. But she was gone! Panic-stricken to think that she might have fallen out of their car, they headed back in search of her. Even though the businessmen retraced their route to the spot where they had picked her up, and saw her tiny footprints in the shoulder of the road where she had first talked to them, they found no signs of their passenger.

Dismayed and mystified, they drove on to Montgomery and found her daughter's name and number in the local phone book. They felt they had to tell her about what appeared to be a terrible accident. After listening to their story in bewilderment, the younger woman pointed to three photos on the mantel. Could they identify their passenger? They did, without a doubt, they had talked to her. They went on to describe her dress, and the daughter burst into tears. That was the dress, she said, her mother had worn when she last saw her.

"When was that?" they asked. The woman replied between sobs, "When she was buried, just three years ago today!"

❋ The Haunted Cabin ❋

Near an eastern entrance to Yellowstone Park in Wyoming, there used to be a crude log shack known as the Haunted Cabin. Here's how it came by that name.

The cabin had long been deserted, when one night, many years ago, a forest ranger camped in it. Just as he managed to fall asleep, he was awakened by a loud pawing and snorting nearby

outside in the snow. It sounded as though some other ranger had ridden up on his horse and was about to enter the shack.

He lay there for several minutes while the noises continued. But no other ranger came to pound on the door. Finally he began to feel uneasy and, taking his gun, crept to the door and threw it open. There was no one there, neither man nor horse.

After lighting a lantern, he circled the cabin, but could find no tracks. Baffled, he went back to bed. Presently the snorting and pawing began again. Again he rose and searched the area around the cabin clearing, but to no avail.

The rest of his night was spent tossing and turning, trying to shut out the loud sounds from outside. The next morning he made still another search, found nothing, and left, glad to be away from the place.

Several other campers and hunters stayed at this cabin during the following months, and all sooner or later reported the same snorting and pawing sounds outside, although none of them had heard any rumors about a phantom horse and rider at the log shack.

Finally, after a restless night, one camper decided to investigate further. He researched the annals of the

Yellowstone area in local libraries and discovered a newspaper account that may—or may not—explain the weird incident, but which was nonetheless intriguing.

The camper learned that many years before the first forest ranger reported the pawing sounds, a drunken cowboy had spent an extremely cold winter night in the cabin. He had tied his horse to the tree by the door and stumbled inside to sleep a frigid eight hours wrapped in his blankets. The horse, left uncovered and freezing outside, pawed and snorted to get free. The next morning the cowboy found his horse dead in the snow.

Perhaps the horse's ghost was still trying to get free from that tree. Or perhaps it was just coincidence that all those who stayed in the cabin seemed to hear the same sounds in the night. The incidents remain strange and baffling.

V. THEIR MESSAGE WAS DEATH

Sometimes ghosts haunt people to get revenge. Some do it just for the fun of it. But a few have appeared for a very specific purpose—to warn someone of approaching death.

The Strangers Who
❋ Foretold Death ❋

One summer afternoon in the middle of the 1800s, a group of boys left St. Edmund's College, a well-known school about forty miles north of London, for a boat ride.

The outing, which began as a happy outing, was to end in grim tragedy. One of the boys, Philip Weld, was to die in a whirlpool in the River Lea—and by some mysterious and inexplicable process, his father, more than two hundred miles away, was to learn of the death at that very moment from two strangers he met on the road.

There were fifteen boys in the group, and they left school shortly after lunch. At about 5 p.m., Philip was rowing a skiff containing three others when they decided to change places. A boy named Joseph Barron was to get his turn at the oars.

Philip stood up and edged his way to the bow, while Joseph took his place. Suddenly, an unseen current seized the boat and swung it violently to the left. Philip clung to the side of the boat, lost his balance, and fell into the river.

Cries of alarm turned to shouts of laughter as Philip reappeared—the water was only up to his waist. Joseph moved the boat over, and the other two boys prepared to drag Philip aboard.

As they reached out, there was a swirl of water and a cry. Philip disappeared before their eyes!

The alarm was raised and other boats arrived on the scene. They discovered that Weld had been standing on a thick shelf of clay that had given way under his weight and dragged him down to the river bottom.

The teacher in charge sent the students home and contacted Dr. James Cox, the president of the college. Workmen with grappling hooks were called out, but they failed to locate the body. Although recovery operations went on until dark, nothing was found.

The next day, a lock farther downstream was

opened, and the movement of the water dislodged the body from its clay tomb.

Dr. Cox did not return to St. Edmund's but travelled to London, and from there to Southampton, to tell Philip Weld's father of the tragedy personally. With a priest, the Rev. Joseph Siddons, he went to Weld's home and saw the dead boy's father walking near the house.

The two men left their carriage and walked toward James Weld. As they approached, Weld said, "You need not say one word, gentlemen. I know my son is dead."

Then he told a strange story. The previous afternoon he had been walking with his daughter along a lane near his house when he suddenly saw his son Philip. The boy was standing on the opposite side of the road between two men dressed in crimson robes.

The daughter exclaimed, "Look—have you ever seen anyone looking so much like Philip?"

Her father replied, "It must be him—it can be no one else."

They noticed as they hurried toward the group that Philip was laughing and talking to the smaller of his companions. Suddenly, all three vanished!

James Weld, certain that the vision signified some impending disaster, went directly home. When the mail arrived, he scanned it with dread, expecting some bad news of his son. But there were only the usual bills and invitations.

"But when I saw you in a carriage outside my gate, I knew without doubt what you had come to tell me."

Dr. Cox asked Mr. Weld if he had ever seen the men in the crimson robes before. He said that he had not, but the faces were so indelibly impressed on his mind that he would instantly know them again.

Dr. Cox then told Mr. Weld of the circumstances of Philip's death—which took place at the very time the vision had appeared.

At the funeral, the father scrutinized all the people who came to pay their last respects to Philip, but the men in the crimson robes were not among them.

Months passed, and James Weld took his family on vacation in Lancashire.

One Sunday, after attending the evening service at the local church, James Weld called on the local priest, Father Charles Raby.

As he waited in the parlor, Weld glanced at the framed portraits on the wall. One, unnamed, pulled him up with a start. The features, the set of the jaw, the shape of the head—he had seen them all before; he knew them as well as he knew his own face. It was the man who had been at his son's side the day he saw him in the lane.

He asked Father Raby about the portrait. He was told it was of St. Stanislaus, a Jesuit saint—the patron saint of drowning men.

❧ Deadly Kindness ❧

It was after midnight in the hospital ward. The lights were dim. A hospital ward at night can be an eerie place—one of uneasy slumber and the restless movement of people in pain.

On this night in September 1956, the women's ward at one of London's most famous hospitals was to have a most unusual visitor—a ghost on an errand of death.

The Grey Lady of St. Thomas's had visited the hospital over a dozen times since the turn of the century. On nearly every occasion, the patient who saw the apparition died soon afterward.

On the night of September 4, 1956, the night nurse heard a gentle tapping on the outer door of the ward. It was 12:35 a.m. Around her, patients were sleeping.

In one corner, in a screened bed, an elderly woman lay gravely and, it was feared, fatally ill. The nurse had been thinking how sad it was that this old lady should die alone with no relatives or friends at her bedside. Then she heard the tapping again, louder this time.

She walked across the room and opened the door. Outside stood a woman dressed in grey. The nurse took her to be a nun.

The visitor whispered the name of the dying woman, and the nurse led her to the screened bed. Ten minutes later she looked around the screens that shrouded the corner. There was no one there—except a corpse.

The patient had died.

Puzzled, the nurse asked the night receptionist if she had seen the visitor leave. "What visitor?" was the reply. "No one came to the wards last night."

The nurse telephoned the night porter. He told the same story: "No visitors came through the gates after 9 p.m." The nurse thought she was overtired. Perhaps she had dozed off for a minute and dreamed the incident.

But the next morning a patient on the far side of the ward caught her arm as she passed. "Wasn't it nice of the nun to come and sit with that poor soul last night?" the patient remarked.

Since then the Grey Lady has been seen at least six times. And death has followed each visit.

Who is she? She is described as middle-aged and wearing a long grey gown. Some say she is visible only from the ankles upward—because she walks on the level of the wards' floors as they were before the hospital was reconstructed.

Others think she is the ghost of a ward nurse who fell down an elevator shaft at the turn of the century. Still others believe she is the wraith of a head nurse who was found dead in her office on the top floor.

But most popular is the belief that she is the ghost of "Morphine Lizzie." Lizzie Church, a nurse at the hospital, had been looking after her fiancé, who had been admitted after an accident, when she accidentally gave him a fatal dose of morphine. Now she is said to appear whenever desperately ill patients are given morphine injections.

Most nurses have a healthy respect for hospital taboos and superstitions. Some will not put red and white flowers together in a vase. To do so, they say, means a death in the ward. And others won't allow white lilies in a patient's room. There is an old hospital belief that they too lead to death.

But not too many of St. Thomas's Hospital nurses believed in the tales of the Grey Lady until one day in 1947. Throughout that afternoon, four nurses working in the women's ward all glanced, at various times, behind a screen that separated off a seriously ill patient. They all saw a nun and two elderly people talking to the woman.

One of the nurses told the head nurse that the patient had visitors, and the head nurse said angrily that she had not given anyone permission to be there.

She went to the ward and found the patient dead, a peaceful smile on her lips—and no sign of visitors.

Later one of the nurses going through the dead woman's effects with a relative saw a small gold locket. Inside were two photographs of a couple she instantly recognized. They were the elderly people she had seen with the nun.

"But that's not possible," said the mystified relation. "They are her father and mother—they both died years ago."

On another occasion, a patient in a men's ward at St. Thomas's looked up, surprised as the young night nurse picked up his water jug. "There's no need to fill it, nurse," he said. "That nice lady in grey has just given me a glass of water." The man pointed to the foot of the bed. The nurse looked but there was no one there. She did not argue. She knew what happened to people who claimed to see the ghost dressed in grey.

The patient, not seriously ill, took a sudden and inexplicable turn for the worse.

He died the next day, twenty-four hours to the minute after the Grey Lady had offered her deadly kindness.

A Lady's Reign
❧ of Death ❧

Three people in the village of Bryanston, near Blandford in Dorset, saw the Lady in White during one long, hot summer, and they lived but briefly to tell the tale.

No one knew whether the Lady in White was real or not; it's doubtful if they ever will. One thing they did know for certain was that she was the harbinger of death.

Early in May, at dusk, farmworker Robert Crewe was walking home when a tall woman dressed in white stopped him in a narrow lane.

"I am looking for the house of Robert Crewe," she told him. "I have a message for him."

"Then you're in luck," he replied, "for I am the man."

"As I said that," Crewe told his wife later, "the lane seemed to suddenly grow dark, and the woman disappeared."

Three days later, Robert Crewe was kicked to death by a horse he was grooming in a stable, and the White Lady's reign of terror had begun.

John Allen, a keeper on an estate near Blandford, spent most of the summer with two other men cutting weeds in the River Stour. He was a cheerful and kindly man, but one night in July he came home from his work and cried bitterly for more than an hour.

His wife, trying to comfort him, asked what was the matter, and Allen replied that he had seen a sign that made him sure he didn't have long to live. He refused to say what he had seen, but remained in low spirits for the rest of the week. He went to work as usual the next day and nothing happened. Eventually, thinking he had been mistaken, he regained some of his good humor and life in the Allen family returned to normal.

The Allens had two daughters, Mary, age six, and Polly, three. At the beginning of August, Polly had been playing in the front yard before she ran into her house with some strange news.

"There was a tall lady in a white dress coming down the hill opposite," she said. "She asked me where my father was and I said he was at the river."

Curious to know who the stranger was, Mrs. Allen went out front. There was no one there. The road leading to the village was empty. Mrs. Allen remarked to her sister, who had come for tea, "Polly must have imagined it—whoever saw a woman dressed in white in these parts on a workday?"

But the child insisted that she had been spoken to by a woman who was "terribly tall, much taller than you, Mother."

As Polly went back out to play, Mrs. Allen glanced at the clock. It was 4 p.m. She put on the kettle and set the table for tea. At that precise moment, the body of John Allen was floating lifelessly in the River Stour.

With two companions named Elforde and Ball, he had been standing in the river cutting weeds from the bank when he slipped and fell into a deep, mud-filled hole in the riverbed. By the time his companions found his body, John Allen was dead. They took the body to a nearby church, and the priest broke the news to Allen's family.

When told of her husband's death, Mrs. Allen immediately said to her sister, "That must have been poor John's spirit that Polly saw."

The rest of the village did not agree with this view. They were convinced the apparition was the White Lady, the malevolent being who brought death to all who saw her.

Their conviction was certainly strengthened when, on September 4, Polly Allen was fatally injured by the moving wheels of a farm cart, into which she ran while playing in the village street.

❧ Face in the Mirror ❧

On a clear October dawn in 1962, Quentin Lloyd suddenly awoke in his hotel room. Something had roused his peaceful slumber. He stared curiously around the room. All was normal. The chimes in a courtyard tower informed him it was six o'clock.

Unable to shake the uneasy feeling, he got out of bed and went to the window. The streets of Edinburgh, Scotland, were deserted, but he knew they would soon be filled with vehicles as the citizens went about their daily routine.

Quentin Lloyd had no explanation for the uncanny feeling that he was being watched, but he knew he was alone in the small room. As he turned away from the window, he noticed his reflection in the mirror on the wall. While staring at his image, the glass became misty and then a new face appeared. It was a face from a nightmare—a terrifying sight with bushy hair, a grizzly

moustache, and glazed eyes that belonged to a dead man. The mirror again became frosted, then Lloyd's own reflection returned.

Lloyd was sure he had seen a ghost. There was no other explanation for the horrifying face. But why had it appeared? Had other guests in this room seen it?

He called a maid and questioned her. She could offer no explanation but said he was the only person to report the apparition.

Quentin Lloyd did not want to spend another moment in the haunted hotel. He packed his bags and went downstairs as a bus was pulling into the courtyard. He was about to step into the vehicle when his blood froze. Lloyd's expression was marked with terror as he stared, completely stunned. The driver's shaggy hair, wiry moustache, and glassy eyes matched the distorted image in the mirror earlier that morning. Without a word, Lloyd hurried back inside the hotel and quickly changed his travel plans.

Three hours later, as Quentin Lloyd sat in the hotel lobby, a maid rushed in to say the bus had crashed. The driver and all ten passengers were killed.

VI. VANISHED!

There is something frightening about the sudden disappearance of people or things. One moment they are there and the next they have vanished without a trace. There are tales of vanishing individuals, ships, planes—even whole towns. Here are a few of the most baffling.

The Man Who
❧ Fell Forever ❧

"Curly" was a sailor who was fascinated by high places. No mast was too tall for him to climb, no cliff too sheer for him to peer over, and no tower too shaky for him to explore. He frequently talked of what a wonderful sensation it must be to fall from a great height.

When his ship dropped anchor at a South American port, Curly was determined to climb an old abandoned stone lighthouse. His friends argued that he couldn't get to the top, and placed bets on him. Another sailor went along with Curly to act as a witness. And so the two entered the musty, damp old tower and started up the crumbling stone stairway.

At last they emerged on a balcony far above the sand dunes. But when they tried to attract the attention of their friends who were playing cards

directly beneath them, their shouts did not carry. Finally, Curly's companion tied his jackknife in his handkerchief, Curly added his lucky coin for weight, and they tossed the little bundle over the rusty iron railing. They lost sight of it as it fell to the depths below, but still did not attract the attention of the other men. Annoyed, they decided to start back down. Curly hesitated a moment. Then with an odd grin he said, "I know a quicker way!" and hurled himself over the old railing, plummeting directly down toward the group below.

The other man screamed a warning and then bounded down the stairs, frantic at the thought of what he would find when he reached the bottom. He burst out the old doorway, hoping that no one else had been hurt by Curly's leap. To his astonishment, the rest of the group was still playing cards, as though nothing had hurtled down upon them from the tower above. Nothing had. Curly hadn't landed!

The group searched the ground for yards around, combing the tower, the dunes, and the water below them, but Curly wasn't there. He was never seen again. They did find the tied and knotted handkerchief containing the jackknife, but Curly's lucky coin was no longer with it. That too, like Curly, had vanished on the way down.

The One They
≫ Couldn't Bury ≪

No one seems to know much about the origin of this tale, except that it happened "way out west" and "way back when." The setting was in a rough-and-ready cattle-raising area where law and its enforcement were often swift and abrupt, though not always accurate. Hangings by lynch mobs were common. They were the almost inevitable punishment for cattle and horse thieves, crop burners, and mine-claim jumpers.

For several months before this incident took place, cattle had been disappearing from the local herds. Suspicion finally fell upon an old codger who lived alone up a canyon a few miles outside of town. He didn't have any cattle, nor could people figure out what he had done with them, but they suspected him all the same. The case against him was simply that no one else was available to blame.

Small groups of men gathered in the saloons and talked about what could be done to stop the thefts. Some of them insisted that they couldn't take justice into their own hands without some proof that the old man *had* taken the cattle. At least, they might try catching him in the act. Others held that they had to hang *somebody* for the crime.

As the cattle continued to vanish, feelings grew hotter, until one day the mob got com-pletely out of hand and headed for the little hut where the old man lived. They found it empty, but as they were leaving, up strolled the old chap, leading his horse. A fresh cowhide was tied to his saddle. There, apparently, was evidence enough that he had been killing cows and skinning them for their hides. This would explain why people had never been able to find any live cattle about his canyon or any other signs that he had been stealing them.

The old codger stoutly maintained his inno-cence. He said that he had found a single dead cow and had skinned it because it did not have a brand on it. The mob examined the hide and, sure enough, could find no brand. But a section of the cow was missing—that part where a brand might easily have been located. This was proof enough for the mob, and they hurried the old man down the mountain to the small town.

In order to make this a spectacle for the instruction of other possible cattle thieves, they decided to erect a scaffolding and hang him in style, instead of just throwing a rope over a convenient tree. The old chap maintained that even if they did hang him they'd never bury him as a cattle thief, and swore long and loud to that effect while they hammered the scaffold together in the town square.

When all was ready and the crowd was waiting, the gang leader sprang the trap. The old man had spoken the truth. He fell through the trap opening but never was actually hanged. The empty noose swung crazily in the air—for the victim had vanished. A cold gust of air whipped over the crowd about the scaffold. Neither the old man nor the missing cattle were ever seen again.

✤ A Walk to the Store ✤

When Sidney Walker left his house on the evening of June 14, 1976, he could not know he would not see his family again until a month later.

The 33-year-old man, who lived in a city near Rio de Janeiro in Brazil, was on his way to a local café for cigarettes and arrived shortly after seven o'clock. After Walker left, the owner realized he had given him the wrong change and hurried outside just in time to see an unidentified glowing object hovering above his customer. The horrified proprietor stood paralyzed as he watched a beam of light engulf Walker, who then vanished.

Sidney Walker's family became worried when he did not return. A few days later, his brother posted a missing persons notice in the local newspaper, *O'Dia*.

Just one month to the day of Sidney Walker's

disappearance, his distraught family received a letter from the missing man, who said he was in Bairro do Dix-Sept Rosado, Natal—more than 1,200 miles away! He explained that he needed money to get home.

Sidney Walker was soon returned to Rio de Janeiro and placed in a hospital for observation. His confused behavior worried his family as doctors performed various tests.

Walker's bewildered condition finally returned to normal and he explained the reason for his long absence. Upon leaving the café on the night he vanished, an unknown force began lifting him. He struggled to free himself but soon became unconscious. He awoke under a grove of coconut palm trees in Natal.

Walker was found by an elderly couple, who invited him to rest in their house. Three weeks later, he recovered his memory and sent a letter to his family.

Sidney Walker had no other recollection of his frightening ordeal.

The Vanishing
❊ Mule Pen ❊

The "mule pen treasure" has produced more frustration than any other lost hoard, because two people have been right on top of it without knowing what was at their feet.

A famous Western badman named Dan Dunham returned from Mexico in 1860, after

several months of looting and robbery. With him were a group of his followers and thirty-one mules loaded with all the loot they had gathered while below the border. As the desperadoes worked their way along the Nueces River six or seven miles below the Laredo Crossing, following a trail on the south side of the river, they were attacked by Apache warriors.

The bandits seemed to be fighting their adversaries off successfully, but it looked as if it would be a long battle. Under cover of darkness the outlaws hurriedly threw up a couple of fieldstone stockades for better protection. One pen was for the mules and the other for the men. They herded the mules into the stone pen, unloaded their treasure from the animals' backs, and buried it in the ground. Then the mules were turned loose to trample the dirt and remove all signs of digging inside the stone walls.

The fight continued for several days. The situation finally became desperate. Dunham decided to go to a fort some miles away for help. Although seriously injured, he finally arrived, but in such bad shape that he gave incoherent directions about where the pens and the rest of his group were.

Weeks later, when he was well again, he tried to retrace his steps. But he never could find the pens. Eventually he died at the fort. No one has ever found the treasure. Yet at least two people have been right there, unaware of the significance of the stone pens.

In 1866, a cowboy named Pete McNeill spent a stormy night in one of them and wondered what such pens were doing out in that wild country. Later, after hearing the story, he tried to find them again—but his search was in vain.

More recently a judge from San Antonio camped near the pens while he was on a hunting trip. Since he had never heard the story either, he did not make a note of their location. Afterward, he too tried to find them and the treasure they held—without success. Others have told similar stories about being on the spot, but no one has ever managed a second visit.

❊ Disappearing Village ❊

Strange things have happened in the long winters of the Far North, but none more baffling than what occurred to an Inuit village in 1930.

A French-Canadian trapper named Joe LaBelle planned to visit friends at a remote Inuit village on the shores of Lake Angikuni. As he drew near the village, he noticed that the usual bedlam of the sled dogs was missing. That was odd, he thought, as he approached the little cluster of low sod huts and crude tents spread along the frozen lake shore. Near the first hut he called a greeting, but no answer came.

He lifted the flap of skin over the doorway on one of the huts and peered inside. It was empty and showed signs of having been abandoned in great haste. He went from hut to hut. All were deserted and all bore the signs of frantic departure. Pots were still full of food. Sewing needles of ivory were left in garments. Even the rifles, so necessary to the people of this northern wilderness, were abandoned, along with food, clothing and personal belongings of all sorts. More than thirty people—men, women, old folk, and infants—had vanished.

On the shore of the lake, Joe LaBelle found three kayaks, including that of the leader of the village, battered by the winds and waves. Seven sled dogs, starved to death, lay by some tree stumps. A grave was open and empty. This was the strangest discovery of all, for opening a grave was unheard of among the Inuit. And to add to the mystery, the stones that had covered it had been removed and neatly piled in two groups beside the open grave. Certainly this could not have been the work of animals or vandals.

Joe LaBelle hurried to the nearest town to

report his discovery to the Canadian Mounted Police. They returned with him to the deserted village and confirmed his story—all the inhabitants had disappeared into the frozen wasteland without a trace, leaving behind the sled dogs and rifles that would have given them their only chance of survival.

Where did the Inuits go and why? To this day nobody knows.

VII. PARTYING WITH GHOSTS

Not all ghosts are frightening. Some of them seem to be enjoying themselves, at least for a while. Others are occasionally downright good company. You'll meet a variety of social spirits in these odd tales.

❧ A Night with the Dead ❧

It happened in the 1890s. A husband and wife driving a buggy along a New England road were overtaken by darkness. Not knowing how far it would be to the next town, they started looking for a place to spend the night. Soon they spotted a light to one side of the road and up a lane through the trees. They turned their tired horse and drove toward it.

The light turned out to be in a small farmhouse on a little hill between two huge elms. The husband rapped on the door, while his wife sat in the buggy.

An aged couple came to the door with a kerosene lamp. When the situation was explained to them, they invited the travellers in for the night. The two couples got along pleasantly, found that they had much in common and, after a warming cup of tea, they all retired. The host refused any payment for the lodgings.

The next morning the travellers rose early to be on their way. So as not to embarrass their host and hostess, they left some silver coins on the table in the hall before they slipped out of the house to hitch up their horse.

Driving to the next town, which proved to be just a couple of miles farther through the woods, they stopped at an inn for breakfast.

Over coffee, they mentioned to the innkeeper where they had stayed the night before and how much they had enjoyed talking with the old couple. The innkeeper looked at them in astonishment. They couldn't have done any such thing, he told them, for he knew the house and the Edmunds who had lived there. The Edmunds had died twenty years before.

The travellers were incredulous. Edmunds was the name the old couple had given them. Their descriptions of the couple tallied with the innkeeper's but the travellers *knew* they had spoken with the Edmunds and had tea with them.

"Impossible," scoffed the innkeeper. The Edmunds had been burned to death in a fire that had completely destroyed their home, and it had never been rebuilt. The argument mounted. Finally the travellers insisted on driving the innkeeper back to the farm to prove they had slept there the night before.

Back they went the two miles. There, to their horror, all they found was an empty cellar hole overgrown with weeds and filled with burned timbers and blackened furniture. The couple could not believe their eyes. Then it was the innkeeper's turn to pale, because with a cry of terror, the wife pointed a shaky finger at a spot in the charred rubble below them.

On what might have been a hall table shone a half dollar and two quarters, just the amount the travellers had left in payment that morning while the Edmunds were still "asleep."

❋ Lucky at Cards ❋

It was a cold and stormy night in the late 1890s. The patrons of the Buxton Inn in Maine were sitting around a roaring fire in the taproom, swapping yarns. Suddenly, a young man entered. His rich clothes were trimmed with gold lace and he carried a cape over his arm. He shook the snow from his tall beaver hat, stamped his booted feet, and strode to the fireplace.

The others looked up with interest, admiring his elegance, but also noting that his clothes were old-fashioned and a bit strange. Undoubtedly, they thought, he was a traveller from some distant city. One of them offered him a place close to the fire, and suggested that he join them in a game of cards. With a cheerful smile he agreed.

As the evening and the game progressed, the young man had uncanny good luck in every deal of the cards. The other players all felt that there was something familiar about the handsome young man, as though they had seen him many times before but couldn't place him. Oddly enough, he knew many of them by name, but never introduced himself.

It was nearly morning when another patron entered. As he removed his coat and boots, he called to the innkeeper. "What's happened to your sign? I thought I had the wrong tavern."

The others, surprised, looked out the window to see the swinging sign outside the door. Wiping the steam from the glass, they saw with astonishment that there was nothing upon the sign but the words "Buxton Inn." The painting of a young cavalier was gone. Then they knew.

With wonder and fright they turned back to the fireplace, but the dapper young card player was gone, leaving nothing but a small puddle of melted snow beneath the chair where his boots had rested. No wonder he had looked familiar.

Almost fearfully they turned again to look at the tavern's sign. Was it a trick of the storm? For now, as clearly as ever, they could see the painting of young Sir Charles in his tall beaver hat and flowing cape, as he had stood for many years. Then something else caught their eye— something they had never noticed before. One of the pockets of his breeches seemed to be bulging as though with many coins, and a smile played about the painted mouth—the kind of smile a young man might wear when he has been lucky at cards.

❊ The Anniversary Party ❊

One night in western Massachusetts, a young man was out with his girlfriend for a moonlight ride on a back road when he ran out of gasoline.

He left his companion in the car and started walking back down the road for help. After going about a mile or so, he saw a light in the distance and hurried toward it.

The light, he soon found, came from a farmhouse set back from the road by a dirt path. He had driven past the farmhouse a few minutes before, but at that time had seen no light.

In fact, the couple had spoken of how sad the old house had looked with its broken windows, hanging shutters, and collapsed porch steps. Perhaps he had been looking at another house, but it *seemed* to be the same.

He walked up the path and took a closer look. Now he was *sure* it was the same house. But what a difference!

It was ablaze with lights. Sounds of laughter and music drifted toward him from across the neatly trimmed lawn. As the boyfriend stood dumbfounded, he heard horses' hooves clattering and stomping. He peered into the side yard and saw about twenty carriages with horses tethered to hitching posts.

That too was strange, for such carriages hadn't been seen in quantities for a half-century. Perhaps the party was a reunion of horse-and-buggy collectors or something like that, he thought. Anyway, they might have some gas somewhere about, so he walked toward a door on the side porch.

On the way, he stopped and looked in a front window. Inside, he saw about forty-five New Englanders dressed in the fashion of 1905, eating and drinking and dancing.

The young man glanced at his watch. It was exactly a quarter to twelve. At that moment a piercing scream came from within, the high-pitched shriek of a woman. And at the same instant the lights went out. He stood stock-still in terror, unable to move or run.

Seconds later, when his eyes adjusted to the moonlight, the young man realized with another shock that he was staring through a broken and dirty window into an empty room. The shutters hung crazily, and the windowsill under his hands crumbled with rot. He turned and fled down the path and back up the road.

When the boyfriend told his story to people who knew the area, they told him that fifty years before, on the anniversary of that night and at a quarter to midnight, a young girl had been murdered in that very room by a jealous lover.

That young man still lives in western Massachusetts, though he is now in his fifties. These days, however, he carries an extra can of gas in his car.

Sam Plays the Ghost
❧ from South Troy ❧

A ghost in South Troy, New York, was a kindly soul who paid dividends in dollars for decent behavior toward him. His story has been circulating for many years now, and while no one seems to know what happened to the people involved, it goes like this.

Although the old house in South Troy was quite well furnished, it was never occupied for long. The tenants always found some excuse for moving out after a few weeks or even days. They said it was too scary to live in, and all gave the same account as to why.

It seems that every midnight a white-bearded old man, tall and thin, came clumping down from the attic and stalked into the parlor, where he stopped in front of some oil paintings and tapped them with his cane or pointed at them. After this he would clump out again and up to his attic. No one could touch him or stop him, but everyone could see him. It was said that if you stood in front of him he would walk right through you and it felt like a cool breeze blowing in your face. He'd never stop, even if the doors were locked shut before him.

Many tenants, as might be expected, told

their stories to Sam, the saloonkeeper at Jefferson and First Streets. Sam never blinked. The landlord was beginning to think he would never rent the place to anyone, when he hit on an idea. He offered Sam and two friends of his a hundred dollars each to spend the night there. Sam, the landlord thought, would see no ghost and would soon dispel the fear in South Troy. Sam agreed and took his friends to the house to play pinochle.

But at the stroke of midnight, the old man did clump down again, and Sam saw him, just as he had been described. Without a word he went to the oil paintings, tapped each with his cane, then started back up toward the attic. Sam stood in his way and got walked through, but it didn't perturb him. It seemed to Sam that the old man was rather lonely and unhappy if he went about walking through people without saying hello.

Sam ran around to the front of the old man and gestured toward the pinochle table, offering him a chance to sit in on a few hands. The old man frowned, puzzled, for a few moments. Then he floated over to the table and sat down. He couldn't hold the cards too well, due possibly to fluctuations in his ectoplasm. Occasionally his fingers would become transparent and the cards would fall to the table. He would seem to apologize. Also, Sam reported, he played a rather naïve game of pinochle. Sam debated whether to throw the game to make the old man happy, but he decided against it.

After a half-hour of pinochle the old man was apparently bored. He rose, banged heavily on the oil paintings with his cane—one, two, ten times—and clumped back up to the attic, nodding politely to Sam, but yawning nevertheless.

After some thought, Sam went to the paintings and took them down. The wallpaper behind them had a fist-size hollow with no plaster behind it. Sam stuck his hand through the paper and pulled out over $50,000 in United States Government Series E War Bonds. He later used them to open a large cocktail lounge on Second and Washington Streets.

The old man continued to be seen, however. It is said he clumps down from the attic even today. All his hoard is gone and he carries no cane or pointer, merely a mournful expression on his face, as if he feels he may have paid too much for a half-hour's entertainment!

The Weekend Guest
⚜ Who Wasn't There ⚜

It was on a June morning in 1936 that Dr. John Rowley, a general practitioner in a rural district in England's West Country, received a letter that led to the strangest episode of his life.

The letter came from Arthur Sherwood, a former medical-school colleague now practicing in London.

"Thank you for your invitation for a long weekend," he wrote. "A spell in the country would doubtless do me a world of good. I will travel by the 10:30 train on Friday."

So it was that Dr. Rowley became involved in one of the most curious and inexplicable stories of the century.

On the day of his friend's arrival, Dr. Rowley had an early lunch and set off for Exeter to meet the London train. Passing a bus stop in his car, he noticed a friend who was an architect, and stopped to give him a lift.

As the station was some distance from the center of town, the doctor invited his friend to meet the train with him. Afterward, he would make a small detour and drop his friend off at his office.

The architect agreed. They arrived at the station five minutes before the train was due and parked the car. Then they walked up to the bridge that spanned the tracks and leaned over it, so they had a complete view of the platform at which the train would arrive.

The train was three minutes early, and only four passengers debarked—three men and a young woman. One of the men was Dr. Sherwood.

"That's him," Dr. Rowley said, pointing to a thickset man in a raincoat and bowler hat.

Dr. Rowley shouted down a greeting. The man looked up, waved, and smiled; then, picking up his suitcase, he hurried out of sight toward the station exit.

Rowley and his companion walked down to

meet him. The other men and the girl came out, but there was no sign of Dr. Sherwood.

"Did the man in the bowler hat already go through?" Dr. Rowley asked the ticket collector.

"Only three people got off the train," he replied. "And they have come through." He held out, as proof, three tickets.

Both the doctor and the architect protested that there was a mistake. They were allowed through the barrier and searched the station buildings for over half an hour, but found no one.

Disturbed and bewildered, Dr. Rowley returned home. He had been in the house just a few minutes when a telegram arrived.

It was from Dr. Sherwood's partner in London—and it reported that Dr. Sherwood had been fatally injured that morning in a street accident soon after leaving home for his weekend in the country.

A telephone call confirmed this was true. Dr. Sherwood had been knocked down by a taxi and taken, unconscious, to a hospital, where he died as the result of a fractured skull.

What possible explanation could there be? Later, at the request of Dr. Rowley, Francis Grafton, the architect who had accompanied him to the station, wrote the following statement:

"It was nearly 10:30 a.m. when I accompanied the doctor to the railway station. The sun was out and the light extremely good. We were standing on the bridge waiting for the train, barely fifty yards from the platform.

"Four passengers definitely alighted from the train—three men and a young woman. Of this, I am quite sure.

"The eldest passenger was a man in a raincoat and bowler hat and carrying a case. Dr. Rowley pointed him out to me as the man he had come to meet. When Dr. Rowley hailed him, the passenger smiled and waved.

"When we got to the barrier, only three people were waiting to come through.

"I am of a skeptical nature, and do not believe in ghosts. Nevertheless, I am completely unable to give any rational explanation of the incident. I confess it is an utter mystery to me."

Is there an explanation?

Psychic researchers call this type of ghost a "subjective" phantom. They suggest that it is a hybrid being, created by the disembodied spirit of the dead person combining with some "piece of matter" to produce a temporary, though very elementary, intelligence.

Other authorities insist that this sort of ghost is a timeless "thought-form" produced by people of the past, present, and future—an image of another world that becomes perceptible to certain people under special conditions.

This, say the experts, was probably what was seen by the men on the bridge—the image of a man who had slipped temporarily into another dimension of time and space.

You may not agree with this explanation. But can you think of any other?

VIII. TALES
OF TERROR

Everyone likes a truly chilling ghost story, but these tales are scarier than most. Better not read them when you're alone in the house.

❖ The Terrible Hand ❖

In 1917, Mrs. Roy Jackson, now of Harrison, New York, went to live in Paterson, New Jersey, with her young husband. They had little money for rent, but they stumbled on an extremely inexpensive house, even for those days.

Mrs. Jackson felt uneasy about the house and at first wanted no part of it, even at twelve dollars a month. Mrs. Jackson's brother, a lawyer who examined the lease, remarked on the dwelling's vaguely sinister atmosphere—saying that he felt a "presence" there that was "not good"—but the rent was low, so the Jacksons moved in.

The months went by and Mrs. Jackson's apprehension grew. Then one day she learned from neighbors that the house was so cheap because it was supposed to be haunted.

A distraught mother had killed herself and her two children in the house several years before. Since then no one had stayed longer than a few days. There were rumors that one of the tenants, and perhaps even more, had been found dead after shrieking, "Someone has me by the throat."

Roy Jackson scoffed at the yarns. He insisted they stay on in spite of his wife's feeling that she was constantly being peered at, followed, and warned to move. Then, on an October night his young wife came face to face with terror and almost lost her life.

The first World War had come, and Roy had begun to talk of enlisting. Mrs. Jackson was lying on a sofa in the living room, thinking about the changes the war would make in her life and looking at a bright spot on the ceiling—a reflection from the gas fixture on the table, she thought. Suddenly she was aware of a second bright spot on the ceiling. Perhaps light from outside? A reflection from a mirror? But there was no other light or mirror.

The spot grew and grew, writhing like "thousands of cobwebs turning and twisting into a mass." A point protruded from the whirling mass, then another and another until she recognized it as a hand with five long, pointed fingers.

Suddenly the mass stopped whirling. Then it grew a long wispy arm behind the fingers, and the entire phantasm darted down from the ceiling, seizing Mrs. Jackson by the throat. With an agonizing lurch, she hurled herself to the floor and lay on the rug, face down, gasping for breath. Moments later she forced herself out of the room to the stairs.

Shaken but unhurt, she finally convinced her husband they should move. One encounter with the grey whirling terror had been enough.

Years later, out of curiosity, the Jacksons returned to Paterson and visited their former landlady. She was in great pain from an old injury. She said that after the Jacksons left, the house had been rented to a single woman. One night she heard screaming and ran up to help— but found her tenant struggling on the floor, choking to death. In her terror, she grabbed the landlady, tearing ligaments that never healed.

❧ A Whistle in the Night ❧

On a small, isolated farm in South Carolina a woman lived alone with her dog. One night, as she was going about her chores, she became aware of an odd whistling sound somewhere outside. It did not sound like high wind in the pines, noises of nature, or a human whistle. It was very strange. Curious, she went to the door. As she did, she noticed that her small terrier was barking and howling on the back porch. This porch, which was enclosed, made a dark and snug haven for the pup.

She opened the door. The wavering and high-pitched whistle seemed to be coming toward the house from across the hills, yet it was as hard to locate as the chirp of a cricket. It must be some of the local youngsters trying to frighten her, she thought, but she shut and bolted the door, and hastily got her late husband's revolver—just in case. She returned to the door to await whatever might be going to happen next. She left the dog on the back porch. If it were just pranksters, his barking would frighten them away.

The whistle came nearer, although the woman could see nothing. Then it seemed to turn, pass slowly around the house, and approach the porch, where the now hysterical terrier was almost beside himself with excitement.

Soon, there was a terrific outcry and sounds of struggle on the back porch. Then silence—as complete as it was terrifying. The woman, alone in the stillness, shook with fright. She did not dare go out onto the porch. Eventually she went to bed.

The next morning she investigated. The dog was gone, and blood was spattered all about. What had taken place? The whistle had stopped when the struggle began. But what was it that had caused the bloodshed? What had happened to the little terrier? Nobody ever found out.

❧ The Strangling Hands ❧

The phantom hands clamped around the child's face, and the room was filled with the chill of death. William Bayles, standing over his daughter's cot, could see the dents in her flesh made by the force of the invisible fingers.

William Bayles and his family had for weeks been terrorized by a presence they called "It," a malignant being that had transformed their cottage near West Auckland, in England's County Durham, into a house of fear. During the spring of 1953 It first arrived at the cottage, where Mr. Bayles, a 40-year-old garage owner, lived with his wife and young daughter.

First, It lurked outside. "We heard a shuffling out in the garden," Mr. Bayles later told investigators. "This occurred for some nights, and then gradually The Thing seemed to nose its way into the house and become mixed up with our lives."

The Bayleses were not easily frightened, but the presence that infiltrated their home filled them with bewilderment, and finally, with terror. Eventually the presence made itself felt every night.

The family couldn't sleep. Furniture was moved, clothes and books disturbed. One night, Mr. Bayles's wife Lottie was grabbed by unseen hands and pulled across the room. Often when the family retired for the night, they found the beds were warm—as though something had already been lying on them.

The family cat refused to remain in the house at night. Mysterious knocks and clatters disturbed even the most sound sleeper.

The final horror came one night when their young daughter, Doreen, was asleep on her cot in her parents' room. Mr. Bayles later described in detail a scene he would never forget.

"First we felt It arrive in the usual way. Everything became chilled and there was a peculiar odor, the smell of a decaying jungle. Then I noticed that Doreen had begun to struggle in her sleep. As we watched, one of Doreen's eyes was forced open and then the other. It was as if someone was forcing them open with a thumb and forefinger. We could see the marks of the fingers on her skin.

"Lottie and I clung to each other, terrified. Then I forced myself to go over to the cot and pry the hands away. I am sure they meant to murder the child.

"I swept my fist over Doreen's face and at once her head fell back onto the pillow, her eyes closed, and her skin resumed its natural folds."

But there was no sleep for Lottie and William Bayles that night. As the dawn was breaking, they vowed that they had suffered enough. If The Thing wanted them to leave their home, they would.

By now, the haunted cottage had become famous. A group of psychic investigators, intrigued by the reports, asked whether they could spend a few days at the place. The Bayles family agreed. They had already found a new home and wanted nothing more to do with the cottage.

In June 1953, two men, equipped with tape recorders and infrared cameras, installed themselves in the haunted room. They locked the door and waited.

A report compiled the next day reads as follows: "We both fell asleep but were awakened by the sound of something soft plopping about on the floor outside the door. There was a silence and then a pawing sound at the bottom of the door.

"We opened the door and dashed out onto the landing. Our flashlights revealed a curious green haze which drifted eerily near the ceiling. We were conscious of a horrible smell, a smell of decay and rottenness.

"We returned to the room and locked the door. We both had the impression that someone—or something—was on watch outside the door the whole night. With the first light the gaseous smell disappeared and the fumbling sounds went away.

"This convinced us that the watcher on our threshold was a creature of darkness and could not face the clean morning air."

The investigators left the cottage none the wiser, leaving an archaeologist to advance the most reasonable explanations of It.

He suggested that the cottage was built over an ancient well that, under certain conditions, gave out a pungent gas that drifted through the floor of the cottage. As it moved, it disturbed the foundations, creating both the smell and the noises.

But why did they disappear at dawn? How do you explain the episode of the "phantom hands"? How were furniture and belongings physically moved?

These are questions no one can answer. The tale of "It" will remain a classic example of the inexplicable—stranger, indeed, than fiction.

❧ Evil on the Cliffs ❧

The chalk cliffs of Beachy Head tower nearly six-hundred feet above the grey water of the English Channel. It is the loftiest headland in southern England, a lonely spot in Sussex in which few people care to loiter—for Beachy Head has a grim history and a macabre reputation.

High among the chalk crags, where the wind always howls even on the balmiest summer day, dwells the most malevolent spirit in Britain. It is an evil influence that, during the past twenty years it is claimed, has hurled more than one hundred victims over the edge to death on the cruel wave-lashed rocks below.

Many have stated positively, some under oath, that they felt this evil influence on the cliffs and had to violently combat a power attempting to force them over the edge to their doom.

Few can stand near the edge of Beachy Head without being aware that some almost hypnotic power lurks in its towering cliffs. A few years ago, a young girl stumbled back hysterically from the Head and up to a patrolling policeman. She said that while she was resting on the cliffs, a cold shadow suddenly descended around her. She felt herself in a strange, dank atmosphere—even though the sun was shining brightly at the time.

She got up and began to run, and "some huge

menacing form seemed to follow me, driving me toward the edge of the cliffs." Screaming for help, she turned and ran away from the cliffs—to safety.

The belief that there is an evil influence luring people to hurl themselves over the cliffs of Beachy Head has been common gossip in Sussex for at least four centuries. Local people agree that the cliffs have a strange and menacing atmosphere. "The soft deceptive chalk seems always waiting to hurl you headlong downward," says a local fisherman.

The influence of the mysterious power extends even beyond the cliffs. A nearby manor house has for centuries been visited regularly by disaster and plagues that have from time to time killed off scores of animals, and even taken their toll of human life.

In fact, it is from this house that the trouble is said to stem. When Britain's monasteries were dissolved in 1538, monks from a nearby abbey took refuge in the manor. The story goes that the owner of the manor betrayed their hiding place. The monks were said to have laid a curse on the man, his family, and his possessions. This, say the local people, is the cause of the malevolence that lurks on the cliffs and in the surrounding districts.

For centuries, people in the district had left the phenomenon alone. But in 1952 a group of people gathered on the cliff top intending to exorcise the evil spirit once and for all.

About a hundred people accompanied medium Ray de Vekey to the top of Beachy Head on a wild night in February. By the light of pressure lamps, they gathered to try to contact the spirits of some of the people who had committed suicide there. But then, in a macabre scene unprecedented in occult research, the medium was suddenly attacked by a presence that urged him to jump over the cliff himself.

De Vekey said afterward that the spirit was fully visible to him. It was an elderly bearded man wearing an ankle-length robe like a monk's habit, with black markings on the back.

"It was in chains," said the medium. "Not handcuffs, but ancient wrought-iron shackles. I don't think anyone could have jumped from the cliffs in chains like that. I imagine it was the spirit of someone who had been bound and thrown from the cliffs centuries ago."

The séance began in the ordinary way, with de Vekey calling on the spirit to make some sign he could recognize.

Suddenly he walked toward the edge of the cliff out of the light of the lamps. The watchers moved forward in alarm.

They heard de Vekey shout, "There is a voice calling 'Oh Helen.' There is a George Foster being called." Then, "Peggy Jordan destroyed herself here …"

"There is a bearded man," de Vekey continued, his voice rising above the wind. "He is evil. He is calling us a lot of blaspheming fools. He is saying he will sweep us all over …"

The medium began to laugh wildly. Four men rushed forward to restrain him from hurling himself over the cliff edge. Apparently possessed, he struggled desperately with his rescuers.

"This thing wants revenge," he shouted. "He wants his own back. He has lain in wait for years." His struggles became more violent; then suddenly de Vekey went limp and was dragged back to safety.

After the séance, de Vekey explained: "This was the strongest influence I have ever encountered. I seemed impelled toward the cliff edge. The specter was of someone who was chained, perhaps the victim of a sacrifice, who has hated and wished ill to all ever since."

A week later, the group again climbed the cliff and de Vekey said prayers. This time nothing unusual happened. The medium said, "I think the unquiet spirit has been laid to rest forever."

But has it? Several years later, two climbers claimed they felt a "malign presence" hovering over them as they walked along the downs behind Beachy Head. Is the mysterious evil thing that lurks high above the sea gathering strength to claim more victims?

What Got
❧ Oliver Larch? ❧

It happened in 1889 on Christmas Eve.

The setting was a farm near South Bend, Indiana. Four or five inches of snow covered the yards and the henhouse roof. Eleven-year-old Oliver Larch lived on the farm with his parents, who were giving a Christmas party for some old friends of the family—a minister and his wife, and an attorney from Chicago.

After dinner, they gathered around a pump organ, and Mrs. Larch played carols while the others sang. She played "Silent Night" and "The Twelve Days of Christmas." Warm voices filled the cozy room, and laughter. After a while, Oliver went to the kitchen to pop corn on the wood-burning range.

At this point, his father noticed that the grey granite bucket used for drinking water was almost empty. He asked Oliver to run out to the well in the yard and refill it. The boy set aside his corn-popper and put on his overshoes. It was just a few minutes before eleven o'clock. It would soon be Christmas, and he wanted to get back to the party quickly.

His father returned to the living room to add his voice to the chorale, as Oliver stepped out into the night—and eternity.

About a dozen seconds after he had left the doorway, the adults around the organ were

stunned by screams from the yard. They rushed out the same door Oliver had used. Mrs. Larch grabbed up a kerosene lamp to light the way.

Outside, the dark, starless night was filled with scream after scream of, "Help! Help! They've got me! They've got me!"

What made the adults recoil in horror was that Oliver's screams were coming from high *above* them in the blackened sky. The piercing cries grew fainter and fainter, and finally faded away completely as the stunned group stared at each other in speechless disbelief.

The men sprang to life, seized the lamp, and followed the youngster's tracks toward the well. They did not get far.

Halfway to the well, roughly 30 feet (9 meters) from the house, the tracks abruptly ended. No signs of a scuffle or struggle, just the end of the tracks. They found the heavy stone bucket about 15 feet (5 meters) to the left of the end of the tracks, dropped in the snow as though from above. That was all.

Oliver had started straight for the well, and then had been carried away—by what? He was too heavy for a large bird, or even several birds, to lift. He was a big boy, weighing about 75 pounds (34 kilograms). Airplanes had not yet been invented. No balloons were aloft that night.

Who, or what, seized Oliver Larch? It remains a mystery that has not been solved to this day, and probably never will be.

IX. SAVED BY A GHOST!

Some ghosts may not be much fun, but they are some-thing better—protective spirits who warn the living of danger. They sometimes even actively save lives. Here are a few intriguing tales of their extraordinary helpfulness.

❧ Lord Dufferin's Story ❧

Lord Dufferin, a British diplomat, is the central figure of this story, which has become one of England's classic tales of the supernatural.

One night while staying at a friend's country house in Ireland, Lord Dufferin was unusually restless and unable to sleep. He felt dread that he could not explain, and so, to calm his nerves, he arose and walked across the room to the window.

A full moon illuminated the garden below so that it was almost as bright as morning. Suddenly Lord Dufferin noticed movement in the shadows and a man appeared, carrying a long box on his back. The silent and sinister figure walked slowly across the moonlit yard. As he passed the window from which Lord Dufferin intently watched, he stopped and looked directly into the diplomat's eyes.

Lord Dufferin recoiled, for the face of the man carrying the burden was so ugly that he could not even describe it later. For a moment their eyes met, and then the man moved off into the shadows. The box on his back was clearly seen to be a casket.

The next morning Lord Dufferin asked his host and the other guests about the man in the garden, but no one knew anything about him. They even accused Dufferin of having had a nightmare, but he knew better.

Many years later in Paris, when Lord Dufferin was serving as the English ambassador to France, he was about to walk into an elevator on his way to a meeting. For some unexplainable reason he

glanced at the elevator operator. With a violent start he recognized the man he had seen carrying the coffin across the moonlit garden.

Involuntarily, he stepped back from the elevator and stood there as the door closed and the elevator started up without him.

His agitation was so great that he remained motionless for several minutes. Then a terrific crash startled him. The cable had parted and the elevator had fallen three floors to the basement. Several passengers were killed in the tragedy and the operator himself died.

Investigation revealed that the operator had been hired for just that day. No one ever found out who he was or where he came from.

❊ The Doctor's Visitor ❊

Dr. S. Weir Mitchell of Philadelphia was one of the nation's foremost neurologists during the latter part of the 19th century. One snowy evening after a particularly hard day, he retired early, and was just falling asleep when his door-bell rang loudly. He hoped it had been a trick of his hearing, or that his caller would go away, but the bell rang again even more insistently. Struggling awake, he snatched a robe and stum-

bled down to see who it was. He muttered in annoyance as he slid the bolt to unlock the door, completely unprepared for the shivering child who stood in the swirling snow.

The small, pale girl trembled on the doorstep, for a thin frock and a ragged shawl were her only protection against the blustering snow-filled wind. She said in a tiny, plaintive voice, "My mother is very sick—won't you come, please?"

Dr. Mitchell explained that he had retired for the night and suggested that the child call another doctor in the vicinity. But she wouldn't leave, and looking up at him with tear-filled eyes, pleaded again, "Won't *you* come, please?" No one—and certainly no doctor—could refuse this pitiful appeal.

With a resigned sigh, thinking longingly of his warm bed, the physician asked the child to step inside while he dressed and picked up his bag. Then he followed her into the storm.

In a house several streets away he found a woman desperately sick with pneumonia. He recognized her immediately as someone who had once worked for him as a servant, and he bent over the bed, determined to save her. As he worked, the doctor complimented her on her daughter's fortitude and persistence in getting him there.

The woman stared at the doctor in disbelief and said in a weak whisper, "That cannot be. My little girl died more than a month ago. Her dress is still hanging in that cupboard over there!"

With strange emotions, Dr. Mitchell strode to the cupboard and pulled open the door. Inside hung the little dress and the tattered shawl that his caller had worn. They were warm and dry and could never have been out in the storm!

✷ The Navajo Guide ✷

A pioneer family of the Old West settled on the edge of a wide forest. In the woods close by lived a very friendly elderly Navajo couple. The Navajos and the little daughter of the pioneer family were particularly fond of each other.

One winter when the youngster was about six, she started walking through the woods to visit another little girl who lived in a cabin about a mile away. She had gone there alone many times

before, so her parents thought nothing of her making the trip again, even though it was winter and it looked like snow. There were few wild animals in the forest, and no wolves had been seen in the area for many years.

A few hours later, when it started getting dark, her parents became concerned. When her father stepped out into the twilight to look for her, he found, to his dismay, that it was snowing heavily. There was no sign of his small daughter.

At once he and his oldest boy bundled up in their heaviest clothes, took a lantern and musket, and started off at a trot down the trail to the other cabin. As they ran along they kept calling the little girl's name, but their only reply was the howling of the wind and an occasional hoot from a great grey owl.

At the neighbor's house they learned that the little girl had left some time ago, before the snow began, and should have arrived home long before. Their alarm mounted. But perhaps, they reasoned, she had left the trail to visit the Navajos' hut.

The girl's brother turned off to visit the

couple, while her father and neighbors headed homeward, fanning out through the dark woods to see if they might find the girl before the snow and storm covered up all tracks.

Reaching home first, the men were overjoyed to find the little girl safe by the fire, drinking hot broth while her mother dried her clothes. She had lost her way, she told them. After stumbling in the drifts for a while, she had started to cry. Almost at once her old friend had appeared and led her home, holding her tiny hand in his all the way, until they could see the lights of her cabin ahead. Then he had smiled at her and vanished into the dark woods behind them.

Her brother returned from the Navajos' hut with a sad tale. There, he said, he had found the man's wife huddled by the body of her husband, who had died two days before.

❈ Death at the Falls ❈

There is a long slim gravestone on the American side of Niagara Falls commemorating those who met their deaths in the raging whirlpool below the falling cliffs of water.

Some died by accident. Others flung themselves over the Falls for fame or money. For others it was a way out of black despair.

A few of them lived for a little while. But Patrick Neil Thompson was not among the elite band. He fell over Niagara Falls one winter night in 1940 and was never seen again—at least not alive.

But how he reappeared two years later, when his son Kenneth was beyond any human aid, is a story that people who live and work within the thunder of the Falls still remember and tell.

Patrick Thompson was a civil engineer. He lived with his wife and son in the small village of Hampstone on the Canadian side of Niagara Falls.

In the late 1930s, the Rainbow Bridge, an old suspension bridge connecting the American and Canadian shores some miles up the Niagara River, had been swept away by ice packs. The company that employed Thompson won the major contract to build a new one.

Construction started early in 1939. It was priority work. The Canadians would soon be at war, and every bridge was needed. The men were working in shifts around the clock to replace the

Rainbow Bridge. Patrick Thompson was in charge of a team of ten men who were working nights under floodlights on a scaffolding platform in the middle of the Niagara River.

On the night of January 17, 1940, Thompson was supervising the unloading of concrete from a barge into a hopper on the rig. A wind of almost gale force was lashing up from Lake Erie, building the waves on the Niagara River into what looked like oceanic proportions. The string of barges in the darkness below banged and rattled against the rig. Thompson stood guiding the crane bucket into the hopper.

Suddenly, the wind caught the crane jib and whipped it savagely to the right. The bucket, at about chest height, caught Thompson, knocking him off the platform into the churning water below.

Five miles downstream the Falls were waiting. He must have been unconscious or semiconscious from the blow because his men heard no sound. Boats were sent out and searchlights raked the water, but Patrick Thompson was never seen again.

An inquest returned a verdict of death by drowning. The Coroner expressed sympathy for his widow and son. The company said it was sorry to lose such a fine man.

Patrick Thompson died the day before his birthday. He would have been thirty-two years old.

Doris Thompson went back to Hampstone and took a job in the office of a building firm. Her son Kenneth, now ten, was going to the local school.

Two years went by. Mother and son were surviving, and it looked as though they were recovering pretty well from the blow fate had dealt them. But fate, it seemed, had not yet done with the Thompson family.

In early April 1942, Kenneth and two friends were on the bank of the Niagara River. Spring thaw had swollen it into a mile-wide torrent. Huge uprooted trees lurched past in the grip of the relentless current. The boys threw small branches into the water and saw them scud away toward the distant roar of the Falls.

Suddenly, Kenneth Thompson, overwhelmed by enthusiasm for the game, grasped a tree bough and tossed it over the bank. With a scream, he lost his balance and toppled into the stream. His two friends watched transfixed as the boy was whirled away.

Incredibly, he did not drown. He clung to the branch, which, bobbing and rearing like a macabre steed, swept him steadily toward the Falls and destruction. His friends, shocked into action, ran to their bicycles and made for the nearest telephone.

The boatmen at Horseshoe Falls prepared their rescue vessels and lifelines but they knew it was hopeless. Water at least forty feet thick was hurling itself over the four-hundred-foot-high curve of rock. Spray lashed hundreds of feet into the air. No human life could persist amid such fury.

Kenneth, on the last bend before the Falls, felt the branch on which he rode speed up like a powerful car. He struggled to keep his head above water. His numb fingers slipped off the bark, and the branch jerked free of him.

As Kenneth sank deeply into the blinding waters, he felt in his heart that he would never rise again. Straight ahead, he could see the semi-circular outline of the edge of the Falls and knew the end was only seconds away.

Then it happened. He felt arms closing around his shoulders. No longer was he drifting helplessly on the current. He could feel the water surging against him, but he was no longer moving. Firmly held by some unknown, unseen force, he began to move toward the bank.

Then he heard the voice. It was low, soft, and heartbreakingly familiar. "Hold on to me and don't be afraid," it said. "I will take care of you."

It was the voice of his father. Of that, Kenneth Thompson had no doubt. Nor had he any doubt that some tangible presence supported him on the hundred-yard fight against the current and helped him up the bank to safety.

Because Kenneth Thompson could not swim.

X. SEAFARING GHOSTS

The seas are mysterious and strange worlds unto themselves. Many things happen on their shores, upon their surfaces, and beneath their waves that are difficult to explain away. The following mysteries of the deep are just a few that have never been solved.

Tale of the Strangled
❧ Figurehead ❧

The Portuguese seamen who tell this weird tale swear it is true.

During the days of the wooden ships and iron men of the last century, a Portuguese sea captain, engaged to a dark-eyed beauty of the Virgin Islands, was determined to have her likeness made into a figurehead for his ship. The girl was flattered by the suggestion, until he insisted that she be portrayed wearing her bridal gown. This, she said, would bring bad luck to them both.

The young captain scoffed at her superstition. How could the figurehead bring anything but *good* luck when she was so lovely and the gown so beautiful? Finally, in tears, the bride-to-be consented and posed for the wood carver in her wedding dress. When the figure was shaped and sanded, she agreed that it was a good likeness, even to the bouquet of flowers she held in her hands.

Amid mixed expressions of congratulations and superstitious anxiety from Virgin Islanders, the figurehead was attached to the vessel's prow under the bowsprit. The young captain sailed off

on a short voyage that would bring him back just in time for the wedding a few weeks later, but the wedding was never to take place.

On the return voyage, a dark high-seas storm overtook the vessel. For days it was touch-and-go as to whether or not she and her captain and crew would survive.

When the storm finally blew itself out, the crew scrambled over the rigging to inspect the damage. To their dismay, they found that a rope had wound itself about the neck of the beautiful figurehead on the prow. They quickly untangled it, but hesitated to tell the young captain of their discovery. However, the superstitious rumors of the crew soon came to his ears. Spreading all available sails, he raced home to his bride-to-be.

A sad-faced group of friends greeted the ship. A tragedy had taken place, they said, and urged the Captain to hurry to his fiancée's house. There her tearful parents told him that his bride had died the night of the great storm. The grief-stricken man managed to ask how, but almost before they told him, he knew.

She had dressed herself in her wedding gown

to have some minor alterations done by the seamstress. She had hurried up to the attic to fetch a bit of silk lace. On the way down the stairs she had tripped on the long skirt and fallen, catching her long, trailing veil on a peg by the stairs. When the parents had found her, she was already dead—strangled by her own wedding veil.

✷ Ghost on the Beach ✷

The Bahamas, vacation islands off the east coast of Florida, have been visited by pirates, phantom ships, and ghosts, as well as by tourists. Great Isaac, a small cay of the group, about a hundred miles northwest of Miami, was the setting for a very eerie visitation.

In 1810, long before there was any lighthouse on Great Isaac Cay, a great storm left tragedy and wreckage behind it. Several ships sank, and many bodies were washed ashore. One of the bodies was a drowned woman who somehow still clutched a living baby in her arms. Rescuers on the cay quickly removed the baby and in time nursed it back to health.

Years later, when workmen were erecting a lighthouse on Great Isaac, one of them met a hooded woman walking along the beach one night. Her arms were outstretched and she was crying, "My baby, my baby!" over and over again.

The workman started to rush to her aid, but then he saw that the rising moon shone right through her figure onto the sand. He stopped in his tracks and rushed back to the camp. Laughter and jeers greeted his story, so from then on he kept it to himself. But not for very long, for he was not alone in meeting the phantom of the beach.

Soon afterward the foreman of the work crew met the same woman, and another workman saw her as well. The laughter stopped. When the

work crew left, they warned the newly appointed lighthouse keeper about her. This was in August of 1859.

From that day on, usually after a hurricane or bad storm, and when the moon was rising, the phantom lady was seen and heard walking the beach.

Then in 1913 she appeared in a most unusual way, as she attempted to climb the stairs of the lighthouse itself.

The keeper was on his way down when he heard her and saw her coming up the spiral stairs toward him. For a moment he was panic-stricken. Then he raced back up the ladder, slammed the trap door behind him, and anchored it down with a heavy crate of machine parts. There he stayed until a full hour after dawn before he dared move the crate away and climb downstairs, half expecting to meet her at every turn.

He requested a transfer the following day, but it was almost a year before the new keeper arrived. He was of sterner stuff and decided to rid the island of the phantom lady for good.

He gathered several Bahamians together around the light and held a solemn funeral service on the beach where the mother and child had originally been found, to put her tortured soul to rest. From that day on there has been no report of the return of the grieving mother searching for her lost child.

❧ Faces in the Sea ❧

In January of 1925, a huge oil company tanker was plowing through the Pacific toward the Panama Canal, when tragedy struck. Two men, overcome by gas while cleaning out an empty cargo hatch, were buried at sea.

Several days later a group of greatly disturbed crewmen approached the captain. They told him an astonishing story. They said they had

seen both the dead seamen following the ship at twilight the past few nights. The captain refused to take their story seriously, but the reports persisted. Even some of the officers saw the apparition.

The heads of the two men would appear in the water off the side of the ship from which they had been cast and would seem to follow the ship for a few moments. Then they would vanish again. Since so many men had seen the apparitions, the captain finally decided to bring the matter to the attention of the officials of the company when they docked in New Orleans.

The company officers listened, disbelieving at first, then with wonder. One of them suggested that the first mate obtain a camera and be ready for the next appearance of the two ghostly faces in the waves. This was done, and the officer gave the captain a fresh roll of film with orders to keep it sealed until the moment it was to be used. The captain promised he would guard the film.

Back through the canal went the tanker, and out again into the Pacific. And once more, at twilight, as the ship reached the same spot in the ocean, the faces appeared alongside.

The captain broke open the film and loaded the camera himself. When the ghosts next appeared, he took six photos and then locked up the camera for safekeeping and away from any possible tampering.

When the ship reached port, the film was taken to a commercial photographer for developing and printing. This man knew nothing about the mystery, nor the reason for the photographs that he processed.

Five of the developed images showed nothing unusual, just waves and spray, but the sixth showed what appeared to be the outlines of two heads and faces in the waves. This photo was enlarged. The objects showed up plainly, appearing in exactly the same relation to the ship as the two ghosts seen by the crewmen and ship's officers.

These photos were eventually inspected by Dr. Hereward Carrington, a noted investigator of psychic phenomena. He checked the story with company officials, and after looking at the photo, reported that there could be no doubt that at least one of the faces in the waves was a realistic photo of one of the dead seamen.

Strange things follow the sea, and not all men go down to the sea in ships. Some wear shrouds.

❖ Skeleton Crew ❖

In 1881, the bark Josepha was sailing in the middle of the South Atlantic en route to Cape Town when the lookout spotted a small vessel some distance away. He aimed his glass and saw what appeared to be a man slumped on the bow.

After hailing was answered with silence, a launch was rowed toward the unidentified craft. But when the seamen reached the drifting relic, they realized that her four-man crew would never be able to tell them what had happened. They were skeletons.

The figure on the bow was still wearing the tattered remnants of an officer's uniform, but it was impossible to determine his rank. His three men, sprawled nearby, presented an even more macabre display, clad in fragments of clothing that crumbled when touched. It was impossible even to tell the ship's nationality, because her name had been erased by weather and salt water.

After studying her design, it was assumed that the ship had been built in England, but there was no flag or insignia to confirm this opinion. The lost ship's destination also remained unknown because her logbook and ship's papers were missing.

The skeleton crew's position—two thousand miles from the nearest land—was no mystery

since winds and currents could have taken them on an aimless journey after the last man died.

What is a mystery to this day is the lonely drifter's fate. How long had the small vessel been manned by a crew of dead seamen? How did they perish? What was the boat's next port? And where was the logbook?

The Mystery of the
❧ *Seabird* ❧

On a strip of land near Newport, Rhode Island, there was a little settlement known as Easton's Beach. Only a few farmers and some fishermen and their families made their homes there.

One day in 1880, a fisherman working on his boat near shore suddenly sighted a full-rigged ship of good size heading straight for land. He thought it very odd that such a large ship under full sail should make no attempt to turn away or head along the coast. But it was coming along steadily and directly in the onshore breeze. He called to the other fishermen nearby and ran to the settlement above the beach to alert the rest of the townsfolk.

Soon everyone was on the beach, watching in helpless silence as the strange ship came on as though determined to wreck itself, its canvas straining and flags snapping at the mastheads.

With horror the spectators heard the grating of the hull upon the bottom as it struck. Yet the ship still bore down, keeping straight on course as it cut a keel groove in the sandy ocean bottom. When it finally came to rest, it was still on an even keel, with the bowsprit almost over their heads.

Then they recognized the ship. It was the *Seabird*, a ship that had sailed under the able command of Captain John Husham. It had been to

Honduras, and its return was expected that very day in nearby Newport. But there was not a sound or sign of life from the decks.

At once the onlookers crowded on board, and the mystery deepened. Coffee still boiled on the galley stove, food for breakfast was on the table, all navigation instruments and charts were in order. Yet there was no trace of the crew, nor any indication of when, why, or where they had gone. The only living thing discovered aboard the ship was a mongrel dog shivering on the deck.

The sea had been calm, the breeze fine, and the *Seabird* had been almost exactly on course for Newport. The crew must have left only shortly before the ship appeared on the horizon. But why should they have left the ship when they were so close to their home and families?

Only heaven and a little dog knew what had happened abroad the *Seabird* that sunny morning.

XI. GHOSTLY ANIMALS

Many people believe that animals can sense the presence of ghosts or other supernatural beings when mere humans are not aware of them. Perhaps it is true. There are many tales about animals who show great fear or love toward someone or something no one else can see. But stories of animal ghosts or animals who are bewitched are a bit less common. Here are a few stories of both kinds.

❧ Night Ride ❧

This story was told by an old doctor who lived a hermit's life in a small New England village. It happened when he was a young boy, but he told it and retold it in exactly the same way until his death.

When the doctor was fifteen years old, his father had a bay colt that he let his son ride. One evening the boy started riding to a nearby town. On the way he had to pass a cottage where a woman by the name of Dolly Spokesfield lived. She was rumored to have unusual powers, skill in the occult arts, and the ability to turn herself into almost anything she wished. She was, it was whispered, a genuine witch of the inner circle— certainly a person to be avoided by anyone out at night alone.

As the lad approached the cottage that belonged to Dolly Spokesfield he kept to the middle of the road and urged the colt to a faster trot. But his precautions were in vain.

As the colt and rider came abreast of the cottage, a coal-black cat suddenly leaped out of the darkness and landed on the colt's neck. The frightened horse stopped short, almost throwing the boy over his head.

The boy tried desperately to get rid of the cat and urged his mount on, beating him with his whip, but the cat held on and the colt refused to

move with the vicious cat hissing upon his neck.

The boy was afraid to leave his horse and run. In panic, he dismounted and began to beat the cat with the whip, holding the colt by the bridle rein as it reared and plunged, trying to shake off the terrifying creature.

At last the boy dislodged the cat and hurriedly rode home. The poor colt was bruised and clawed, and apparently exhausted by his ordeal. So injured and frightened was he that the boy was afraid the animal would die before morning. He turned him loose in the barn instead of putting him in the stall, and went to bed trembling and fearful that the colt wouldn't last the night.

At dawn, the boy hurried to the barn to inspect the battered and clawed animal. To his amazement, the young horse was in perfect condition. He showed no sign of exhaustion, and nowhere on his body could the boy find a trace of bruises from the whip, a claw mark, or a single reminder of the frantic events of the previous night.

The story has an even stranger ending. A

neighbor soon stopped by to report that Dolly Spokesfield had just been found almost dead, her body bruised and beaten as though by a whip. And under two of her fingernails were some short bay hairs, such as you'd find, perhaps, on the neck of a young colt ridden by a frightened boy alone in the night.

The Witch Cat of
➤ the Catskills ❖

Spook Woods, a strange spot in the Catskill Mountains of New York State, deserved its name.

It was said that even dull-witted cattle who wandered into these woods would suddenly rush away in panic at what they had encountered. Certainly horses often balked at taking the road that ran through Spook Woods. The local people

usually managed to go through it only in broad daylight, and preferably with company.

A farmhand named Williams, the story goes, had been hired to work on a farm on the other side of the woods from his home. Williams had heard tales of Spook Woods, as who up that way hadn't? But he was a big, rugged, and ordinarily fearless man who paid little attention to tales of witches and supernatural happenings.

However, one winter night as he returned home through the woods on foot, he did feel a certain uneasiness. It was only because of the full moon that cast odd shadows along the side of the dirt road, he reassured himself. But as he reached the center of the wooded stretch, he realized that one shadow was hurrying along *ahead* of him. This shadow was more than a trick of moonlight, for it was moving quickly over the snow along the roadside.

As he hurried to pass it, he saw to his astonishment that the shadow was made by two cats who were dragging another, obviously dead cat, between them. What a strange way for animals to act, he thought, as he quickened his steps. The cats hurried too and kept right up with him. Then, to his increasing horror, one of them called him by name.

Startled, he wouldn't—he couldn't—stop. The terrified man began to run, desperately anxious to get out of the woods as fast as possible.

The cats, slowed down by their burden, were unable to match his speed, but just as he was leaving the thick woods for the open country beyond, one of them screeched in a loud, clear, and almost human voice, "Mr. Williams, oh, Mr. Williams, when you get home tell Molly Myers that she can come home now. Old Man Hawkins is dead."

Terribly shaken by his experience, Williams raced home. Once he reached its warm, friendly atmosphere he hesitated to tell anyone about his harrowing experience. But later in the evening, when sitting with his family around the fireplace, he half-jokingly told about it, and finally repeated the odd message.

To everyone's astonishment, the old white cat lying by the hearth sprang to her feet, and without once looking back, leaped up the chimney right over the burning logs and was never seen again. Was that Molly Myers? Had she at last gone home?

❧ Haunted by a Dove ❧

Many years ago, in an Alabama village, there lived a man and his wife who were supremely happy together. After years of wedded bliss the wife became very ill and nothing could be done to save her.

On her deathbed she announced to the family and servants that she would return to the garden in the form of a white dove so that she could be with her husband in the place where they had

known such true love and happiness. Moments later she died.

Years passed, but no dove appeared to carry out the dying wife's promise. Eventually the widower fell in love with another woman and decided to marry her and bring her to the big house to live.

On the day he carried his new bride over the threshold and into the house, a white dove came fluttering into the garden and perched upon a flowering snowball bush by the gate. It uttered long, low moans as though it were heartbroken.

Every afternoon the dove returned to moan and sigh on the snowball bush. The servants were frightened and upset. They thought that surely this meant that the first wife's promise was now being carried out!

Eventually the second wife heard the story, and she too became disturbed. Soon people from the village and from neighboring plantations came to stare over the garden wall at the dove on the snowball bush.

The new wife grew nervous and ill-tempered, and the happy home began to crumble. Legend or no legend, the husband wanted to preserve his new life. Frantic, he decided upon drastic action.

The next afternoon he seized his rifle and slipped from the house, stealthily working his way into the garden, where the dove sat moaning and sobbing. He raised his rifle and fired. A woman's scream answered the blast of the gun and the dove flew away, its breast reddened with blood.

That night, as the husband slept, he died. No one could determine the cause. His widow moved away to escape the tragic memories, and the great house fell into ruins.

The master of the house was buried by the snowball bush. His gravestone, they say, is still

there, but there are no visitors—but one. For it is said that every spring when the blossoms of the snowball bush first open, a white dove with a red-splotched breast appears among them, moaning pitifully.

The Case of the
❧ Kitten Ghost ❧

It lies in a special file in the Paris headquarters of the French Society for Psychical Research—a photograph of a small boy in his Sunday best, holding a pet kitten in his arms.

The kitten is small and white, with huge, appealing eyes set in a tiny face. It had been given to seven-year-old René Leret in August 1954, and from that moment on, the boy and the little cat were seldom apart. René even took the kitten to school—at least until the teacher objected. It slept on his bed, and often sat on his knees at mealtimes.

"If anything happens to that cat, I dread to think what René will do," remarked Michelle Leret to her husband one night. "It would break the boy's heart."

But when that day came, there was no grief in

the cottage on the edge of the village of Sampier, near Lyons in southeastern France. For it seemed that not even death could separate René Leret and his pet.

The events at Sampier, at first written off as a small child's fantasies, soon attracted the attention of France's top ghost hunters.

"I have studied well over two thousand cases in

the course of my career," wrote Dr. Gerard Lefeve of the French Society of Psychical Research, "and only five times have I failed to put the supernatural into natural terms. One of these was the case of the kitten at Sampier."

It was August in 1954 when René's uncle came to visit, bringing presents for everyone, including the tiny kitten for René. Immediately, the child christened it Jacques, and took it with him everywhere.

But the friendship—at least in normal terms—was to last only a month. One Saturday morning the kitten suddenly dashed through the garden into the main road. An oil truck on its way from Lyons to Dijon dashed the life from the tiny scrap of fur.

The parents kept the boy away from the scene until all traces of the accident were removed. "You must not be too sad about Jacques," Michelle Leret gently told her son. "We will get you another little kitten to take his place."

"I don't need another one, Mother," the boy replied. "Jacques is here sitting by the window."

He reached out to stroke the air a few inches above the window ledge.

The parents regarded the action as a defense mechanism shielding René against the grief of losing his pet. Doubtless it would disappear in a couple of days.

But it didn't. Jacques had to have his food put out as usual; the door had to be opened to let him in; the cushion on which he had slept had to be in its place on René's bed.

One day, Charles Leret told his son gently but firmly that the pretense had gone on long enough. The child was bewildered: "But what do you mean? Jacques is here on the carpet—can't you see?"

The next day the worried parents called a doctor and told him their child was suffering from hallucinations. But examinations—culminating in hospital tests—could find nothing mentally wrong with the child.

Dr. Lefeve, hearing of the phenomenon, arrived at the village at the end of September. He had several long interviews with the child and his parents, and he carried out several routine tests. He found that when the child entered the room, the temperature appeared to drop slightly—always a sign of a "presence."

Examining the inside of the front door, he found minute scratches around the bottom, apparently made by cat claws. Yet the door had been newly painted—after the cat had died.

Then there was the photograph. Dr. Lefeve was in the Leret house when it came back from the local pharmacy. The folder containing prints from a roll of film taken by Charles Leret was opened and the contents casually examined. There were pictures of the house, the family, and the garden.

And there was a picture of René, taken near the garden gate.

Charles Leret's hand shook as he handed the picture to the doctor. It showed René, in his best clothes, looking strangely solemn. In his arms was a white kitten.

"The parents were astonished," Dr. Lefeve recalls. "When the photo was taken, there was no kitten or anything else in the child's arms. I examined the photograph and there was no doubt that the object was a kitten.

"I asked the parents every question I could think of, and they answered willingly and honestly, but they could not throw any light on the mystery."

And no one ever has. For the picture of René Leret had been taken three weeks *after* Jacques the kitten had died.

A Horse Named
⇒ Lady Wonder ⇐

The two men could barely keep a straight face as the stable door opened and out shuffled the oldest, boniest horse they had ever seen. This clinched it! Now there was no mistake: The whole thing was a hoax.

On the face of it, the feelings of the men who stood in the stable yard in St. John's, Newfoundland, Canada, in 1955, would have been echoed by anyone with normal healthy skepticism. For they had been persuaded, despite their better judgment, to seek advice from this pathetic creature on the fate of a missing child.

But within minutes, what appeared to be a joke in rather bad taste was transformed into an uncanny glimpse into the supernatural that no one has ever been able to explain.

It soon became obvious that only one being in

the whole of Canada knew what had happened to three-year-old Ronnie Weitcamp. And that was Lady Wonder, a thirty-year-old mare, spending the twilight of her days in a stable a hundred miles away.

On October 11, 1955, Ronnie left his three playmates in the front yard of his home near a Newfoundland naval base and ran around to the

back of the house. He disappeared into some nearby woods and, despite the pleas of his playmates, wouldn't come out. As they ran to tell his mother, the child roamed deeper into the woods.

Neighbors scoured the woodland. By midafternoon, the police had been called and a full-scale search mounted. As darkness fell, 1,500 searchers combed bushes and ravines. The bitter cold descended. They knew that if the child was not found, there was little chance of his surviving the night.

But he wasn't found, and the police, convinced that their search had been thorough, turned to other theories.

Had he been kidnapped? Eleven days passed, and there was no sign of the child.

The tips and leads supplied by the public led to nothing, and hope was almost abandoned. Then a police official remembered that a child had been found years before, through information supplied by a horse!

In any other circumstance it would have been laughable, but the police looking for little Ronnie Weitcamp had become desperate. Just as the searchers were nearly defeated by despair, two detectives were sent to interview the horse.

By any standards, Lady Wonder was a remarkable horse. By the time she was two years old she had learned to count and spell out words by moving children's blocks around.

One day she spelled out "engine" as a huge tractor rumbled past the house. Later, in response to questions, the horse would use her nose to flip up large tin letters that hung from a bar across her stall. In this way, she spelled out the answers to questions put to her.

The fame of the horse had spread. Thousands came to seek answers to their queries. She was claimed to have predicted that Franklin D. Roosevelt would be the next president of the United States, before he had even been nominated.

She picked the winners of countless races, and venturing into the field of mathematics, briskly calculated the cube roots of numbers. University specialists in extrasensory perception spent weeks testing the horse and came away convinced that she had some kind of telepathic powers.

But she remained basically a harmless curiosity until one day, after a four-month search for a seven-year-old-girl, the police turned in desperation to Lady Wonder. She directed them to a water-filled quarry that already had been searched without success. A further hunt led to the child's body, exactly where the horse had indicated.

Coincidence or not, in the absence of any other idea it was worth trying. But now the horse was old and such tests upset her. After convincing the owner that this was an emergency, the officers were eventually allowed to question Lady Wonder.

The bar of letters was put in place and the questions began. They asked, "Do you know why we are here?" Immediately the horse spelled out "boy."

Q: Do you know the boy's name?
A: Ronnie.
Q: Is he dead or alive?
A: Dead.
Q: Was he kidnapped?
A: No.

Q: Will he be found?
A: Yes.
Q: Where?
A: Hole.
Q: What is near him?
A: Elm.
Q: What kind of soil?
A: Sand.
Q: When will he be found?
A: December.

That was the end of the interview. Refusing to answer any further questions, the mare tottered away. The detectives telephoned headquarters with the answers and a new search was discussed.

A storm of ridicule descended as it became known the police were acting on the advice of a horse. Naval base officials, particularly, insisted that the ground had been thoroughly searched and it was quite obvious that the child had been abducted. However, a new search took place, nothing was found, and the police department began to curse the day they sought the help of Lady Wonder.

Then on the afternoon of Sunday, December 4, the body of Ronnie Weitcamp was found by two boys in a thicket at the bottom of a ravine about a mile from his home. He had not been kidnapped: Medical evidence showed he had died of exposure. He lay in sandy soil, just out of the shade of the nearest tree—a large elm.

Every detail of the horse's prediction had been proved uncannily accurate; it was unbelievable but true. It was also the last time Lady Wonder used the swinging letters.

The following spring, she died, taking with her the mystery of her glimpse into a world few humans have ever penetrated.

The Creepy Chicken of
❧ Pond Square ❧

Don't laugh too fast. A chicken may not sound scary, but what if it were the ghost of a chicken, gruesomely killed as part of a scientific experiment?

This ghastly ghost dates back to the 1600s—a time before people knew much about how things live, before DNA tests, and test-tube babies, and heart transplants.

People who conducted scientific experiments often dug up graves to study the bodies of dead people. This activity, and the knowledge that came from it, was both startling and frightening to "normal, decent folks," who felt one shouldn't question why people live and breathe.

Back in 1626, scientist and philosopher Sir Francis Bacon observed that grass appeared to die when covered by a thick blanket of snow, but would come back to life when the snow melted and spring began. As a scientist, he wondered— would an animal also die if it were surrounded by snow, but then live again shortly thereafter? In order to find out, Bacon killed a chicken, ripped out its organs, and stuffed it with snow.

But Lord Bacon never had the opportunity to find out whether the chicken would come back to life. Handling the snow gave the scientist a chill. He took very ill and died a few days later.

Strangely, the body of the chicken disappeared from the scene without any explanation.

While there have never been reports of Lord Bacon's ghost being sighted, there have been countless sightings of the creepy chicken's bizarre little spirit. Hundreds of accounts by witnesses throughout the ages tell about an eerie, ghostly chicken in Pond Square, England. At the site where the chicken was murdered, it can be seen feebly hopping and flying in circles, and then disappearing right before witnesses' eyes!

XII. STRANGE!

Strange thumps and bangs, transparent figures floating through the wall, or shrieks in the night can scare the living daylights out of any of us! What you are about to read are among the creepiest, scariest ghost tales ever recorded. Could these weird tales possibly be true? Those people who recounted the stories assured us that they were. Some even claimed to have been witnesses. What do you think?

The Light
❧ in the Window ❧

On a train traveling west through Canada one night, some of us were sitting up pretty late telling yarns. One fellow told this story.

A friend of his who lived in Ontario once became fascinated with an old painting he saw in a dingy little store. It showed a dramatic-looking castle on a hilltop. The scene was dark, mysterious and gloomy. Every window in the castle was dark—except for a small, arched casement high in a stone tower. The man wondered why anyone would paint a castle with a light in just one window. Was there a story behind it?

He bought the painting and hung it in his home, but all the storekeeper could tell him was that it depicted a castle in Scotland. There was neither signature nor date.

One day, as he was cleaning the painting, he found a few Latin words in a corner. He asked a friend to translate the words, and learned that they meant "every century it will be dark." This inscription made little sense to him, and he forgot about it.

The painting hung in the man's home for many years. Sitting around after dinner, he and his friends enjoyed speculating about who was in the tower and why the window was lighted. It was quite a conversation piece.

One evening the owner of the painting was telling some guests about how he had acquired it, and answered questions about its background and meaning. The guests wanted to see this unusual and mysterious piece of art, so they all trooped into the hall where it hung.

Imagine their astonishment and the consternation of their host when they saw that, on the painting, the window in the tower was dark!

Examining the painting closely, they were astounded to see that the black paint on the once light-yellow window was as old and cracked as the paint on the rest of the picture. There were no signs that it had ever been different, let alone bright yellow.

After the guests had gone, the embarrassed host unsuccessfully tried to find a solution to the puzzle. The next morning he returned to the painting and felt his skin crawl. The window in the tower was lighted! Then he thought of the Latin inscription, "Every century it will be dark." He made a note of the date and began a serious search into Scottish history.

Eventually these facts were uncovered: The

castle had been the home of an evil character who had two sons. He hated the elder son and kept him locked in the tower, while his younger son enjoyed all the wealth and pleasures his father could give him.

Exactly five hundred years before the night when the painted window had gone dark, the imprisoned elder son had died in the little room high in the tower.

The Old Man of
❊ the Woods ❊

Presque Isle, Maine—one of the most remote
spots in the United States—is perhaps for this
reason the setting for many peculiar legends and
tales. One resident reported the following weird
incident during World War II.

Near the spot where this man's father had
lived when he was a boy, there was a Presque Isle
family with two children—a boy and a girl.

The youngsters had no friends to play with in the deserted area, so they had to invent their own games and entertainment. They often took walks in the nearby woods.

One day the children began to talk about a nice old man who lived in a cabin back over the hills. At first, the parents were concerned. But no one knew of any such man, nor could his cabin be found. They decided the old man had been dreamed up by the children to make up for their lack of real friends—so they didn't give the matter much thought.

As time went on, the children began to report on some things that the old man said would be happening to the local residents, their livestock, and their crops.

Strangely enough, almost all these dire events took place.

People lost their crops, their livestock died, and folks were taken sick—just as the children's friend had said they would.

The parents of the youngsters didn't approve of the morbid interest in death and destruction their children were displaying. And so, the children were refused permission to visit the woods anymore, although they continued to sneak away whenever they could.

Finally the parents delivered an ultimatum: The children would bring the old man home to meet their family, or they would be forbidden ever to see him again.

The boy and the girl said they would invite their friend, but they were not sure he would come. Off they went into the woods, with the parents laughing as they waited—assuming there was no such person at all, but marveling at how their offspring could have departed so full of confidence.

They soon found out.

A half-hour later, the children returned. A tall bearded man—obviously very old, but with a strong, active stride—was with them. He was strangely dressed, in a suit of black material that had twinkling glints of gold here and there. His battered hat appeared to be made of a special black fur felt. His beard was pure white, and his blue eyes were piercing.

He greeted the parents pleasantly, and they

were soon reassured that their children had indeed found an interesting and unusual friend.

After staying for a while, the old man bade them farewell and asked if the boy and girl could walk back with him to the edge of the woods to say good-bye. The parents agreed, and the three started off, the man holding the youngsters by their hands.

As the little band walked toward the sunset, the parents were startled to see that only the children cast a shadow—there was none for the bearded man who walked between them. Their awareness came too late, however.

Neither the old man nor the children were ever seen again.

The Creepiest
❧ Confession ❦

In the early 1800s, an unsuspecting Mexican priest heard a dreadful confession ... from a dead man. The encounter, which occurred in Mexico City, proved to be the most tormenting experience of the priest's life and went down in history as one of the creepiest confessions ever told.

One stormy winter evening, Padre Lecuona hurried through the stinging rain to the house of a friend. On his way he heard the voice of an old woman call out to him: "Padre, please wait. You must hear a confession. It is urgent, we haven't a moment to lose!" The priest, eager to arrive at his destination, answered, "Surely one of the other priests can attend to this matter."

"Oh no," declared the woman. "He asks for you—and only you!"

The woman led the padre to a dilapidated, darkened house in an alley. As he followed her through the door, a wave of foul air assaulted him. The woman lit a candle. In the flickering glow, he could see the form of an emaciated man lying flat on his back on the floor in the corner.

As the priest knelt down, he sensed something was wrong. The man's skin was brown and

leathery, stretched tightly over bones. The head was but a skull scarcely covered with skin and a few wisps of matted hair.

"Mother of God!" gasped Padre Lecuona. "This is no living man!"

Suddenly, the figure rose to a sitting position and croaked, "Forgive me, Father, for I have sinned." In a raspy voice, the corpse recounted how, years before, a gang of thieves had broken into his home, stolen all of his possessions, and murdered him and his wife with a hunting knife. Because he died so quickly, he was never able to receive his last rites by a priest.

Now, the man claimed, through divine intervention, he had been permitted to return and make his confession.

Horrified at what he was seeing and hearing, the priest quickly forgave the man for the sins in his previous life. When he was finished, the man crumpled into a mummified corpse. The priest fled the house at once and began looking for the old woman in hopes of getting an explanation for the bizarre occurrence, but she had disappeared.

The next day, still in shock, Padre Lecuona and a friend returned to the house in the alley. The door looked as if it had not been opened in years. Cobwebs stretched over it, even over the rusted keyhole.

Could the entire incident have been a dream? Distraught, the men broke into the house. Inside they saw only a vacant room. "Hello?" the men called, but their voices echoed through the empty house.

As Padre Lecuona turned to leave, he saw a handkerchief lying in the corner where the corpse had been. It was the one he had been carrying the night before. As he bent to pick it up, a sharp pain shot through his chest, and a wave of dizziness engulfed him.

"Are you all right?" the priest's friend asked in alarm.

"I think so," answered the padre, but those were the last words he ever spoke. The priest clawed at the door, opened it, and then stumbled out into the alley.

Three days later, after lapsing into a state of delirium, the padre died. Doctors were never able to find a cause or reason for his tragic demise, but when the house was demolished years later, a moldy, crumpled, mummified skeleton (the corpse who confessed?) was found behind one of the walls.

The house where the supernatural confession took place sat in an alley in Mexico City. Soon after the padre died, the townspeople dedicated the alley to the priest by naming it Callejón del Padre Lecuona (meaning the Alley of Father Lecuona), which it is still called today. It is said to be a dark and dangerous place, haunted by evil spirits.

Mrs. Reeser's
⚘ Strange Death ⚘

Fire, a great blessing from the days of the cave-man on, occasionally sets off mysteries that are as difficult to believe as they are to solve. This was the case in the 1951 death by burning of Mrs. Mary Reeser of St. Petersburg, Florida.

This elderly lady lived alone and was last seen alive by a friend the night before her unusual death. Her friend went to call on her again at about eight o'clock on the morning of July 2, 1951, to take Mrs. Reeser some coffee and a telegram.

To her astonishment, the friend found the handle of the door too hot to hold. In alarm, she ran for help. Some carpenters who were working nearby returned with her and forced open the door to Mrs. Reeser's room.

A ghastly sight greeted them. The room was

almost unbearably hot, although the windows were open. Close to one of the open windows were the charred remains of a chair—and of Mrs. Reeser herself.

All that was left at that spot was a small pile of blackened wood and a skull, several coil springs, and a few bits of bone. Another small pile of charred wood marked where an end table had stood, and a burned floor lamp lay some distance away.

The room itself was strangely affected by the fire. Above a line three or four feet from the floor, the walls and curtains were heavily coated with black soot, as were the screens of the open windows. A base plug in the wall had melted, short-circuiting a lamp and a clock that had stopped at 4:20 a.m. A small wall-type gas heater was turned off—and was untouched by the fire, although there had been such terrific heat in the room that a pair of candles on one table had melted and run out of their holders onto the table itself.

Under the pile of charred wood and bones there was a burned spot on the rug. But nothing else had caught fire.

What happened in that room may never be known. The arson experts from the police department and Board of Fire Underwriters, as well as the doctors, could not determine what had caused such terrific heat and such strange reactions to it.

It was estimated that temperatures up to 3000Þ F (1650Þ C) would be required for such complete destruction of a body and a chair—and not even a burning body, clothing, and wood could generate that temperature, even for a short time.

There had been no lightning that night. Experts determined that no explosive fluids or inflammable chemicals had been present that could raise the temperature of a typical household fire to the degree at which such complete cremation could take place.

A mirror on the wall was cracked and candles melted. Why hadn't other things in the room caught fire? Why wasn't the house destroyed as it would have been in an ordinary fire? Why did it stay so unbearably hot in the room until eight in the morning, even with the windows open?

This was no ordinary fire and no ordinary event. But what was it?

XIII. FAMOUS GHOSTS

Even in the world of apparitions, stars can make their mark. Some of the people who were famous in life have returned to claim a new kind of recognition as ghosts. Here are some stories of those who have done just that. Is the limelight so hard to give up?

Not Gone with
➤ the Wind ➤

One magnificent mansion in Atlanta is among the few antebellum homes to escape the disastrous fire during the Civil War. It was unharmed by General William Sherman as he marched through Georgia in 1864.

The stately house was built on three-hundred acres of woodland five years before the first shot was fired at Fort Sumter in April 1861.

Many ghosts have dropped in on this house, but the most famous visitor is the author whose epic novel about the Old South became a classic motion picture in 1939.

The spirit of Margaret Mitchell first appeared in the spring, several years after she sold the house. She had intended to help the new owner restore the antique mansion but died in 1946, when she was hit by a car.

Margaret Mitchell had wanted to preserve the elegant estate that served as a model for Tara in *Gone with the Wind*.

On her first ethereal visit "she came through the closed door," said the owner. "Now she comes every year, carrying flowers and wearing a green dress. She never speaks. Instead, she always has an armful of jonquils as she wanders through the house."

After the first time the owner saw the famous author's ghost, he went to visit her grave. Her plot was covered by a bed of jonquils. Perhaps she wants to remain in the house that in life was so dear to her heart.

The Beautiful Blonde
≫ of Brentwood ≪

Once upon a time, a lonely teenage girl named Norma Jean Baker left her foster home and became a model. A few years later, she was earning seventy-five dollars a week as a contract player at 20th Century Fox. Norma Jean would soon become Marilyn Monroe and eventually a screen legend in her own time, as a beautiful Hollywood movie queen.

On August 5, 1962, the world was stunned to hear that the blonde goddess had died in her home on Helena Drive in Brentwood, a suburb of Los Angeles, California.

Marilyn Monroe had a lifetime interest in the supernatural. She often consulted astrologers and psychics for reassurance and comfort during frequent periods of depression and unhappiness.

One morning around 12:15, a couple was driving through Marilyn's neighborhood on

their way home. As they passed the star's former home, they slowed down when a blond woman, wearing white slacks and loafers, suddenly appeared on the lawn. When the apparition came closer, the curious pair recognized the woman as Marilyn Monroe. She continued walking toward the car, and then disappeared.

Some have seen Marilyn make her way across the lawn, then move near a tree and clasp her hands. Others have seen her glide from the house and into the street before fading away.

Unlike most dwellings of the rich and famous in Beverly Hills, the enigmatic star's house was not a grand mansion on a landscaped lawn. The modest, single-story home featured small rooms and privacy. A coat-of-arms adornment placed near the front door announced, *Cursum Perficio*, which means "I am finishing my journey."

The proverb came true.

Marilyn Monroe loved her Mexican-style house—the only home she owned during her life—and it may be the reason she came back to visit, after her death.

Washington Irving
❧ Returns ❧

Libraries are wonderful storerooms for books offering adventure, romance, and mystery. The Astor Library in New York also offers a famous ghost.

In 1860, Dr. J.G. Cogswell was working there late one evening when he heard a sound a few aisles away. He got up, walked around a bookcase, and saw an old man reading at a table.

The stranger looked familiar, but Cogswell could not identify him in the sparse lighting. As he approached the shadowy figure, he realized he was looking at his old friend, Washington Irving, who had written over a dozen literary classics.

There was only one thing wrong. Washington Irving had been dead for several months, and

Cogswell had been a pall bearer at Irving's funeral!

As Cogswell began walking toward his friend, the ghostly figure vanished.

A few nights later, Cogswell was again working alone in the library when he saw his dead friend hunched over a book. The glowing, white-haired phantom seemed oblivious to Cogswell and disappeared before the doctor could speak.

Cogswell finally told his friends about the supernatural visit and was advised to spend a few days relaxing in the country.

But he was not the only person to see the famous author.

Pierre Irving, the writer's nephew, saw his uncle at the family residence in Tarrytown, New York. The apparition appeared in the parlor and walked to the room where Washington Irving created *Rip Van Winkle* and other masterpieces.

Pierre stared quietly at his uncle's spirit. He was as shocked as Ichabod Crane meeting the Headless Horseman. Moments later, the hazy image faded away.

Ironically, the author of *The Legend of Sleepy Hollow*—America's first ghost story—did not believe in the supernatural. He would probably be amused to learn that he would become the most celebrated ghost in New York.

✳ Blackbeard the Pirate ✳

The pirates of old were legendary, larger-than-life characters who lived at sea on ships that they often stole from innocent people trying to make their way to new lands.

Few pirates were more feared than Edward Teach, otherwise known as Blackbeard the Pirate.

Captain of his own ship, Blackbeard punished his men harshly and didn't hesitate to shoot or throw overboard a disobedient sailor.

His murderous, plundering life caught up with him in 1718, when Lieutenant Robert Maynard of England's Royal Navy surprised Blackbeard at the pirate's favorite cove—Ocracoke Inlet, off the coast of South Carolina.

Maynard and his men laid a trap, and the evil Blackbeard sailed right into it. Within minutes, Maynard and Blackbeard were locked in combat, dueling hand-to-hand in a fierce sword fight. The hulking Blackbeard snapped Maynard's sword in

half, leaving him helpless. When the pirate raised his cutlass to finish Maynard off, one of Maynard's loyal men snuck up from behind Blackbeard and cut his throat.

Legend has it that even while blood spurted from his neck, Blackbeard kept fighting. It took an additional five shots and twenty stab wounds to finally lay him to rest. Fearing the ferocious pirate might come back to life, Maynard had Blackbeard's head cut off and hung from the ship's bow.

The sailors said that when Blackbeard's body was dumped into the ocean, the head cried out for it and the body swam around the ship three times before sinking.

Ever since, Blackbeard's ghost has haunted the area of his bloody death. Fishermen have reported an eerie, glowing, headless body floating just below the surface of the ocean. And sometimes, around Ocracoke Inlet, Blackbeard's ghost ventures ashore in search of his head!

So what happened to Blackbeard's severed head? After it hung from the bow of Maynard's ship, the head was taken apart. Blackbeard's skull was then coated with silver and used as a most grotesque punch bowl.

❧ As Time Goes By ❧

Most of the ghosts who once haunted the ancient buildings in New York City were evicted long ago, when the shabby structures were replaced by modern glass and steel skyscrapers.

One building that escaped a demolition crew's steel ball was the Manhattan Opera House at 311 West 34th Street. Rousing operas are no longer offered on its stage, and the archaic structure is now called Manhattan Center. It serves as an auditorium for political rallies, business meetings, and conferences.

Many years ago, an obscure immigrant's dream to stage operatic sensations came true when his widely acclaimed productions of *Louise*, *Electra*, and *Pelléas et Mélisande* were presented at the theater he had built in 1906. Oscar Hammerstein had accumulated a fortune when he invented a cigar-making machine that allowed him to pursue his dream.

An old theatrical producer insists that Hammerstein's spirit has often been seen by unsuspecting visitors.

One man who is not afraid of the mysterious events at the theater is the custodian. When he took the job, he was asked if he believed in ghosts. He assured the management that he did not and was hired on the spot. He replaced a

young man who had been terrified by unusual sounds and scenery props that seemed to move by themselves.

"Once in a while these big pieces of scenery are found here on the stage," said the custodian. "They are stored against a brick wall across the room. No one ever hears a noise, but those heavy flats do move around, and it usually takes three big men to handle them."

When asked if he had seen the ghost of Oscar Hammerstein, he smiled, and said, "I don't look for nothin' and I don't see nothin'. I do hear weird noises, but this is an old building."

Those who have seen the impresario, who died in 1919, say he appears to be content as he sits in the lower right-hand box, staring at the empty stage, as though his operatic triumphs were being performed.

❧ A Gift from Beyond ❧

Mrs. Patrick Campbell was the first actress to play Eliza Doolittle in George Bernard Shaw's Pygmalion. When her fame began to fade into pleasant memories, she was nursed through a period of illness by another actress, Sara Allgood.

If ever a name suited a person, Allgood was a perfect match for Sara. Her kind expression made her a natural for the motherly roles in which she often appeared. She had acquired a reputation as a great actress long before she left her native Ireland for the bright lights of Hollywood.

When Mrs. Patrick Campbell had recovered, she was grateful for the wonderful care provided by Miss Allgood and presented her with a water-color painting of a heron.

Sara Allgood moved to California in 1940, and her first dream in the new house was puzzling. Mrs. Campbell appeared, and said, "Have you found my gift from the grave? Look behind the picture."

Allgood was confused and had no reason to believe the aging star had died. When she removed the cover behind the watercolor of the heron, she found a caricature of Mrs. Campbell by Sir Max Beerbohm that was worth about two thousand dollars.

Sara Allgood later learned that her benefactor had died on the day of the mysterious dream.

I. BIZARRE!

Almost everyone has experienced some peculiar feeling or event, or heard a fantastic tale from a thoroughly reliable source. And when it happens to you—or to someone you trust—the occurrence is hard to ignore. Even when it is bizarre.

The Ghost of Dead
❊ Man's Curve ❊

In 1908, a trolley line in New York State ran from Port Chester to Rye Village and Rye Beach. The tracks crossed one road that was really just a right-of-way raised up over a swamp. A hand-operated switch at the crossing point could throw the trolley on either of two routes.

This swampland was full of tall reeds, cattails,

pools of dark evil-smelling water, and, reputedly, quicksand—a highly unlikely place for human beings to venture. But apparently one unfortunate person did. Or did he?

Late one night the trolley rocked and clattered down the tracks to the crossing point. The motorman stopped and got down to throw the switch so that he could proceed toward Rye. There were two passengers in the huge, dimly lit car, one man seated at each end. Neither man paid any particular attention to the other.

After the motorman had climbed down to the switch, one of the passengers also got up and left the car. The switch was thrown. The motorman came back to his post, and the car started along, picking up speed.

For some time the remaining passenger did not realize that the other man had not returned. When he did, and told the motorman, the trolley was almost in Rye.

The motorman reported the lost traveler, and a search party was quickly organized, for the swamp was known to be treacherous. But neither that search party nor one formed the next day could find any trace of the missing man.

Where could he have gone?

The most logical explanation was that the man, probably a stranger, had set off across the swamp and perished in one of the bottomless pools, or in quicksand. Nothing, certainly, was ever seen or heard of him again.

From then on, until the trolley line was discontinued, that crossing point in the swamp was known as "Dead Man's Curve," and people gave it a wide berth on dark nights or gloomy days. Those who did occasionally walk along the tracks often reported low moans, faint calls for help, whistling, and splashing from deep in the marshland.

Perhaps they were the natural voices of the swamp, the calls of birds, or the moaning of wind in the bulrushes ... or perhaps they were the regretful cries of the shade of an ill-fated traveler, who stepped out of a trolley and into eternity.

The Haunted
❧ Schoolhouse ❧

The small schoolhouse in Newburyport, Massachusetts, was the scene of a strange phenomenon in 1870.

Every day a mysterious yellow glow spread over the classroom, windows, and blackboards. It usually started near the hall door and spread silently over the room. After about two minutes it faded away. It did no harm while it cast its light over the room, but afterward the students and their teacher, Miss Lucy A. Perkins, felt weak and ill.

The yellow radiance was not the only unusual occurrence. It was accompanied by a gust of cold air that swept through the room, even when the doors and windows were tightly closed. The chill breeze rustled the papers, swung the faded map on the wall, and shook the hanging oil lamp.

This too, made the teacher and children feel slightly ill, but Miss Perkins kept the class going day after day, bravely trying to ignore the strange event.

In the late fall, the yellow light disappeared and a low-pitched laugh was heard. The eerie sound echoed in the school's tiny attic, the small coal cellar, and the hall. One day, many of the students, along with Miss Perkins, saw a child's hand floating in the air. Then the arm became visible.

The climax came on November 1.

During a geography lesson, Miss Perkins called upon a student to recite. In the midst of a sentence he suddenly stopped and pointed to the hall. There stood a boy with his arm upraised. It was the same arm and hand that had floated in the air.

The mysterious boy stood silently, his face bound in a white cloth as though he had an injured jaw or a toothache. Then, as they watched, he slowly vanished.

From that time on, the schoolhouse was plagued no more.

In an attempt to solve the mystery, the authorities questioned three local boys who had a reputation for mischief, but they decided the trio had no part in the events.

To this day, the yellow glow, the cold breeze, and the boy with the upraised arm and bandaged jaw have never been explained.

❧ Voices of the Dead ❧

On a warm summer evening in 1949, the four children of Captain and Mrs. Roland Macey finished their high tea in the paneled dining room of Fresden Priory, a rambling mansion that had once been a monastery.

The children ran through the open French windows and out onto a small flagged terrace where their mother was sitting with the local priest.

"Mother," said the oldest child Mary, who was twelve years old, "can we go upstairs and listen to the singing?"

"What is that?" the priest inquired.

"Oh," said the mother, "they say they can hear singing up in the nursery, but of course it is all nonsense."

It turned out, however, that what the Macey children could hear was anything but nonsense. It was what psychic researchers call a "mass echo in time," and certainly the most uncanny and well-documented example of "voices from the dead" ever reported.

For years, authorities on the paranormal had sought proof for the centuries-old belief that antique furniture or wooden altars used for mass had the power to transmit through time the Latin chanting of monks who lived hundreds of years before. Now, it seemed, the

four Macey children were going to provide that proof.

The priest asked permission to accompany the children up to the nursery. There he saw a large table standing against a wall. The children stood beside the table and immediately became completely absorbed.

Although the priest could hear nothing, he asked them to try singing along with what the children called the "funny music," and they did.

When he returned downstairs, the priest told Mrs. Macey, "What your children can hear, but we cannot, is the sound of the monks who lived here 500 years ago, singing their evening office. It is archaic plain-chant Latin, completely unused today."

The children knew no Latin, were not Roman Catholic, and had never even heard a Latin mass. So when they repeated what they had heard "the table singing," there was no way to doubt them.

But children, it seemed, were the only ones privileged to hear the chanting monks.

A team of experts arrived with high-frequency recording equipment and heard nothing. The table itself was examined and carefully taken apart, revealing a false top. Underneath was a wooden frame with a stone cross set in it.

It was an altar used for secret masses when Catholicism was illegal in England.

Dr. William Byrne, a medical student with a fine reputation as a psychic investigator, heard about the singing at Fresden priory. He asked for and was granted permission to visit the house. Once again, the children repeated the words they heard coming from the table. Some teenage cousins visiting the house also claimed that they could hear the singing.

Late one evening, after making a series of unsuccessful tests in the house, Dr. Byrne and two assistants were walking across the drive to their car when they became the first—and last—adults to hear the voices of the dead.

"We heard," Dr. Byrne was to explain later, "the sweet singing of ghostly monks. It was so clear on the air that at first I thought it was a radio turned on. But it was not. Then I realized we were below the window of the room in which the altar stood.

"For over half an hour, the chanting continued. Almost afraid to move, I reached out to switch on a portable tape recorder I was carrying.

"Suddenly the singing stopped. Then I heard the voice of a man slowly reading. The voice came from the thin air about twenty feet from me and was in some archaic form of Latin."

Then there was silence. Dr. Byrne clicked off his recorder and wound back the tape. The spools revolved—and only a quiet hiss emerged from the speaker.

The voices were, it seems, beyond the range of any man-made equipment.

How *can* the past be transmitted to us through inanimate objects?

Roger Pater, a well-known expert on the occult, explains it like this: "Anything that has played a part in events that aroused very intense emotional activity seems to itself become saturated, as it were, with the emotions involved—so much so, that it can influence people of exceptional sympathetic powers and enable them to see or hear the original events almost as though they had been there."

Is this the explanation for the phantom voices of Fresden Priory? It probably is—at least until someone can think of something better!

❈ The Flying Monk ❈

This question has baffled scholars and churchmen for nearly three-hundred years: Could St. Joseph of Copertino fly in the air?

The incredible exploits of this 17th-century Italian monk were seen and vouched for by close to a hundred witnesses—including a pope. But absolutely no clue as to how they were done can be found in the written accounts of his flights. Had St. Joseph actually discovered the secret of how to overcome gravity?

By any standards, he was an extraordinary man. From the age of twelve he wore a hair shirt next to his skin and a heavy iron chain drawn tightly around his waist. Frequently he fasted for long periods.

As he grew older, Joseph became even more serious and strict. By the time he joined the Order of St. Francis in 1625 he was no longer content to wear just an iron chain about his waist, so he attached a large metal plate that tore at his body.

Stories began to circulate that he possessed supernatural powers. These tales became so widespread that he was ordered to Naples for questioning by the Holy Office.

He was examined three times. The fourth time, he begged to be allowed to say mass in the Inquisition's own church of St. Gregory of Armenia. A few moments later, startled onlookers were hardly able to believe their eyes.

Rising in the air, Joseph floated over the amazed congregation. He then flew to the altar where he alighted amid the flowers and burning candles.

Nuns in their place behind a screen called out,

"The candles! The candles—he'll catch fire!"

But Joseph's robes did not catch fire, although the flames from the candles licked them several times. After a few minutes, he rose into the air again and flew back into the body of the church.

The court of the Inquisition rushed him off to Rome to have an audience with the Pope. As he entered into the presence of the Pontiff, before a word had been spoken, Joseph drifted up into the air and remained suspended for fully a minute.

Later, he was sent to a monastery in Assisi. One Christmas Eve, a party of shepherds was invited to his church to play music upon their pipes.

The shepherds had barely begun their performance, when Joseph began to dance, suddenly gave a great sigh, and flew like an angel onto the High Altar. He remained there for about twenty minutes, again in the midst of flaming candles. Then he flew down again and blessed the shepherds.

On another occasion, Joseph was walking with the priest Antonio Chiarello when he suddenly flew across the garden and came to rest on top of an olive tree. Chiarello was amazed to see that the branch that bore Joseph's weight was hardly as thick as a man's finger.

Not content with "solo flights," St. Joseph began to take other people with him. His first "passenger" was the father confessor of the Convent of Santa Chiara in Copertino. During a festival, Joseph grasped his fellow priest by the hand and rose up with him into the air.

One of the most extraordinary demonstrations of Joseph's strange gift occurred when he came upon ten laborers who had collapsed upon the ground, exhausted after hauling a huge cross of solid walnut.

"What is the matter, my children?" Joseph asked. The men explained that they were so tired they found it impossible to drag the great cross the last yards to the spot where they had to erect it on the crest of a hill.

The monk took off his cloak and ordered them to stand aside. "I am here!" he cried, rushing toward the cross.

Then, as though it weighed only a few pounds,

he flew with the cross, carrying it right over the laborers' heads, and set it down in the hole that had been prepared for it.

Even on his deathbed, on September 17, 1663, Joseph amazed everyone present—including his doctors—by rising from the bed and flying as far as the little chapel of the monastery.

The story of his ability to fly was vouched for scores of times, by the most eminent and respectable of witnesses. All were satisfied that he used no mechanical tricks. But St. Joseph of Copertino went to his grave taking his secret with him.

XV. MAN'S BEST FRIENDLY GHOSTS

Dogs can be fun pets, loyal companions, protectors, and even seeing-eye guides. But can dogs also be possessed by spirits from the other side? Read about some ways that man's best friend has been haunted in these next tail-wagging tales.

❋ The Dream Dog ❋

Retired Colonel Elmer G. Parker, of Riverdale, New York, had a most unusual dream some years ago, on the night of a snowstorm. Unable to sleep, he had come down to the living room in his robe and slippers, poked up the logs in the fireplace, and settled down on a couch in front of the fire.

A few years before, when his beloved Irish setter was alive, Laddie liked sleeping on that same couch, but at no time during the evening had the Colonel thought of the dog.

Presently Colonel Parker fell asleep and dreamed vividly. The dog came to him and touched his knee, first with his nose and then with his paw. It was Laddie's sign that he wished to go out. The gentleman did not remember dreaming that he got on his coat and hat, but simply that he got up, took the dog's leash, opened the door, and went out with him into the snowy street.

He dreamed that the dog ran down the steps and across the yard, rubbing his nose in the newly fallen snow, while Parker walked behind, having let him off the leash to run. For some moments Laddie raced about. There was no one on the deserted street, or at least not in the dream. Then they returned to the house and the Colonel once more lay down on the couch to sleep.

About five-thirty in the morning Colonel Parker woke up feeling cold. The fire had gone out. He discovered that the door to the living room was wide open, not as he had left it.

He reached down for his slippers and found them soaking wet. Startled, he hurried to the front door and found the entrance hall was also wet. He looked out the front door onto the stoop and down across the snow-covered yard.

There were his slipper prints in the fresh snow, down across the yard and back again, and beside them, both going and coming, were the clear footprints of a large dog—about the size of those made by an Irish setter.

❧ The Frightened Dog ❧

Tom grew up in North Carolina, where he often went hunting in the woods and swamps, bringing along two of his friends, and his dog.

One day they set forth with their guns, planning to be gone only a few hours.

Late that afternoon it began to rain very hard. Since they were far from home, the boys decided to spend the night in an abandoned shack they

had stumbled upon, rather than try to find their way home in the dark.

The shack was empty except for some rubbish, a few old clothes, and a lantern that still had some kerosene in it. Eventually the boys fell asleep on the floor, with the dog curled up beside them, while the rain splattered upon the roof overhead.

During the night they were awakened by the dog whining and scratching at the door. He was trembling violently, and the hair on his back was raised as though he were frightened or angry.

Rather sleepily, one of the boys started for the door to let the pup out. Then he froze in his tracks. From the black woods outside the shack came a weird, startling sound. A combination of whine, low moan, and rising and falling wail, it was like nothing the boys had heard before anywhere.

They stared at each other, then reached for their rifles as the dog raced around the room, barking and whining, and showing his teeth.

One boy quickly lit the lantern.

The window openings of the shack contained no glass but were covered with mosquito netting. Suddenly the dog hurled himself through one of these openings and ran off into the woods, snarling and barking.

The three boys waited with hearts pounding and .22's clutched in their hands. At last the strange sound faded away in the distance and they heard nothing but the patter of the rain on the tin roof.

A few minutes later the dog leaped back through the broken netting and came toward them, whining and shaking, with his tail tucked between his legs. He was a very frightened white dog. That was the most amazing part of the adventure, for when he had left the shack to run into the woods after the "thing," his coat had been black!

❧ Drip, Drip, Drip ❦

This eerie encounter is said to have taken place around West Chazy in New York State.

Not long ago a local resident, deciding to go fishing in a nearby pond, dug himself some worms, cut himself a nice pole, and taking along his dog, clambered into an old flat-bottomed boat for a quiet afternoon.

The dog curled up in the bottom of the boat and fell asleep almost as soon as the man had baited his hook and tossed it over.

The fish weren't biting. The man rowed from one spot to another, trying first here and then there along the shore. It was almost as though all of the fish in the pond had been caught or were in hiding.

Finally the man decided to try his luck in the middle of the little lake, where the water was deepest. The moment he anchored there, the dog, who had been sound asleep the whole time so far, woke with a start and began to whine and tremble.

The man spoke sharply to him, telling him to be quiet and lie down. The dog obeyed, but he kept whining softly and trembling violently.

Hardly had the man dropped his hook to the bottom when he felt a tug. He began to pull on the line, but it seemed to hold fast to the bottom.

At this point, the dog jumped to his feet and

began to bark viciously, showing his teeth and peering over the side of the boat, rocking it sharply. While struggling with the line, the man gave the dog a blow with one of the oars, sending him into the other end of the boat, where he cringed, whimpering.

Once more the man heaved his stout fishing pole. Slowly his catch—whatever it was—came to the surface. Tangled on the end of the line was a great clump of what looked like human hair. Shining in it was a bright golden barrette.

As the object appeared at the side of the boat, the dog let out a howl of terror and plunged into the lake, heading for shore. He soon made it to land and vanished into the woods.

The man was amazed at the actions of the dog, but nevertheless decided to take the hair home and give the barrette to his wife. She could use it, he thought, to hold her hair back.

The barrette was so entangled that they would need to hang the hair before the fire to dry out to make removal easier. His wife, though horrified at the idea, coveted the bright barrette and so consented.

Long after the strands of hair were dry, the sound of dripping could still be heard.

It went on all evening. Then, at the stroke of twelve, a woman's voice came from the hanging strands. It told of her murder and how her body could be recovered. Then the voice faded away and was heard no more.

The man and his wife couldn't believe what they'd heard and decided to keep it to themselves for the time being, particularly so that the wife could keep the valuable barrette.

However, the dripping sound continued. It went on all night and all the next day, and the day after that. Finally, they could stand it no longer and reported their find to the authorities. Police dredged the lake and recovered the body, which was identified by the golden barrette.

The dog never returned.

Ghost Dog on
❧ the Stairway ❧

A ghost dog was seen in 1929, not once but several times, and not only by humans but by dogs as well.

One human who saw it was Pierre van Paassen, world-famous author of *Days of Our Years.*

In the spring of that year, van Paassen was living in Bourg-en-Forêt in France. One night he was startled to see a black dog pass him on the stairs of the house in which he was staying. It reached the landing and disappeared.

Van Paassen searched the house, but could not find any sign of the dog. He assumed it must have been a stray that had wandered in and out again.

A few days later he left on a short trip, not thinking much more about the dog on the stairway.

When he returned, however, he found the

household greatly upset. During his absence several others had also seen the black dog, always on the stairs.

Van Paassen decided to stake out and watch for the ghostly animal the following night. For corroborating witnesses, he invited a neighbor, Monsieur Grevecoeur, and his young son to join him.

Sure enough, the same black dog appeared at the head of the stairs. Grevecoeur whistled, as he would at any ordinary dog. The dog wagged its tail in friendly fashion.

The three men started up the stairs. To their amazement the black animal began to fade and it vanished before they could reach it.

A few evenings later van Paassen stood watch again, this time accompanied by two police dogs. Once more the ghostly canine appeared, and this time came partway down the stairs before it vanished.

A moment later the two police dogs seemed to be engaged in a death struggle with an invisible adversary, and presently one of the huge dogs fell to the floor dead. Examination failed to reveal any outward signs of injury.

This was too much for the owner. He called in a priest to advise him. The Abbé de la Roudaire arrived and watched with van Paassen the next night. When the black dog appeared the priest stepped toward it. The beast gave a low growl and faded away once more.

The Abbé at once asked the owner of the house if there was a young girl employed there. The owner admitted that there was, but also wanted to know why the priest had asked. Did the good Abbé think that there might be some connection between the young girl and the mysterious apparition?

The Abbé shrugged his shoulders and said there was sometimes an affinity between young people and some types of mysterious happenings. The girl was dismissed—and the ghost dog on the stairs was never seen again.

XVI. SPIRITS WITH A MISSION

Could a nurse still be saving the lives of her patients, after her tragic death? Could a starving crew, lost at sea, be rescued by the commands of their dead captain? Find out in these tales of ghosts who came back to the world of the living—to fulfill a mission, tell their stories, or complete unfinished business.

The Spirit of
❧ Lindholme ❦

During World War II, the Royal Air Force station at Lindholme, England, was not your average fighter base, and British pilots were not the only airmen who flew deadly missions against vital targets in Germany.

There were aviators from many nations based at Lindholme, but the most maniacal of the bunch were from the Polish air force.

Polish fliers lived only to destroy German planes and cities to retaliate for the deaths and incarceration suffered by their families at the hands of the Nazi troops. The eager airmen would fly until they were ready to drop from fatigue, then take off as soon as they awoke from a few hours of sleep, refueled on hot coffee.

One pilot from this highly driven crew perished in a fiery crash, but still would not quit.

One evening in 1945, a Halifax was returning to Lindholme. The encounter had been successful for the enemy. German antiaircraft gunners had severely damaged the heavy four-engine bomber.

But the plane was not the only victim of the attack. The pilot was seriously injured, bleeding from several wounds and barely managing to keep the airplane level as it approached the field.

Time became another enemy. As the minutes ticked away, the wounded pilot was getting weaker. He found he was having increasing difficulty concentrating on what he knew would be the one chance to land the bomber.

Then time ran out.

Just as he saw the lights of the airfield, the pilot knew he could no longer maintain altitude. He decided to attempt the landing alone and ordered his crew to bail out. When the last crewman cleared the plane, the desperate pilot lined up with the runway. The plane hit the ground heavily and created a giant watery rooster tail as it began skidding.

Whether it was because the brakes failed or

the pilot lost consciousness, the huge bomber came to rest in a soggy bog. Moments later, it had completely disappeared, sunk into the marsh. The operations officer added the aircraft to his long list of casualty statistics, removed the dead pilot's name from the daily schedule, and the war continued.

The Halifax was gone forever, but the valiant aviator refused to be taken off the duty roster.

A few weeks after the tragic crash, the base chaplain was startled by an unusual sight. A pilot, wearing a ragged flight suit and bleeding profusely, suddenly appeared and asked for directions to the mess hall. The chaplain wanted to take the wounded airman to the dispensary, but the ghastly figure utterly vanished before he could speak.

On another occasion, an officer was approached by a bloody flier in a torn flight suit who asked for directions to the mess hall—then disappeared.

The war ended, but the late Polish airman still continued with his unrelenting search for the Lindholme mess hall. The gruesome specter was seen for years, until local authorities decided to claim the bog for its peat deposits.

A digging crew discovered the remains of the Halifax while clearing the marsh. The properties of the bog had preserved the bomber and its lone crewman. The pilot's body sat in the cockpit, dressed in the same ragged flight suit seen by so many at the airfield during the past forty years.

He was buried with full military honors and never seen again.

Rebel from Nashville

Hypnosis has been a mystifying attraction for eager crowds at circus sideshows and carnivals for decades. Many skeptics are surprised to learn that it is also a legitimate technique used in modern medical practice, dating back to the 18th century.

The procedure can be performed in many ways, and it allows the subject to block out everyday sights and sounds and focus on a particular goal.

One November afternoon in 1957, a young secretary named Patricia Kord had been hypnotized by her uncle, Richard Cook. He used the technique to treat her for chronic headaches. Normally Patricia would lapse into a relaxed state and her painful headaches would be temporarily eliminated without the use of expensive medication.

This session would be very different.

As his niece Patricia slipped into a deep hypnotic trance, Richard Cook began to notice that her breathing was getting slow and laborious, and her pulse was rapidly dropping. He had quickly decided to bring her out of the trance when the young secretary began to speak.

But the voice belonged to a stranger. The tone was definitely masculine, and the words came slowly.

"My name is Gene Donaldson," claimed the voice from her lips.

Cook was astonished. This had not happened before during any hypnotic session he had ever conducted. He was intrigued by the unexpected voice and began to question the unknown entity.

"Who are you, Gene?"

"I was in the Confederate Army and fought at Shiloh."

"How long have you been a soldier?"

There was a pause. "I was working at my folks' farm near Shreveport when a wagonload of men passed by. They were going to enlist and I went with them. They put us on a boat and went down the Red River. I was in the fight at Shiloh and lost an eye to a Yankee shot."

"Were you in any other big battles, Gene?" Cook asked. He wanted to learn as much as he could and did not know for how long he could communicate with the former soldier.

The voice described numerous adventures that ended during the battle of Nashville, where he was killed in action.

The hypnotist investigated the unusual claim

and was rewarded. He found answers he never anticipated. In reviewing volumes of Confederate Army records in the National Archives, he found evidence to confirm the soldier's story.

In May 1861, Private Eugene Donaldson had joined the Louisiana Volunteers and participated in the battle of Shiloh on April 6–7 the following year.

Official documents confirmed that Private Donaldson was killed in December 1864 at Sly's Hill, the scene of a minor skirmish during the battle of Nashville.

Cook also reviewed county records and learned that a Donaldson family had owned property in Shreveport, Louisiana, as far back as 1811. Other details described by the late rebel fighter were also confirmed.

What wasn't confirmed was how the spirit of Private Gene Donaldson managed to reveal itself through a twenty-eight-year-old secretary who used hypnosis to ease her dreadful headaches.

✳ The Phantom Captain ✳

He was a tall, broad-shouldered man with an unmistakable air of command, a barrel chest, and a vivid scar that curved across his temple and down his left cheek. On a January night in 1902, the men in the wheel house of the James Gilbert all saw him clearly.

They felt the blast of spray as the tall man forced open the wheelhouse door and spoke to them as they struggled with the buffeting wheel. The three-masted ship was beating through monstrous waves on the 4,600-mile run from the Cape of Good Hope to Bombay.

The order given by this stranger with captain's rings on his sleeve saved the lives of seventy-four men who were within a few hours of a hideous death from starvation and exposure. But at the very moment the crew saw him and heard him speaking, his body was floating lifeless on the storm-tossed waters of the Indian Ocean.

Of this there is no doubt. Nor is there any doubt that the story of the phantom captain is one of the strangest of all inexplicable tales of the sea—still discussed when sailors gather to swap yarns.

The *James Gilbert* was forty years old when it sailed into marine history. Its square rigs and jaunty profile made for a picture-book ship, and when conditions were right, it could still outrun

most of the new-fangled steamships riding the watery routes.

In midwinter 1902, the *James Gilbert* left London with sixty-eight officers and crew, and fifteen passengers bound for Bombay. Captain Frank Carter was in command.

In a heavy overcoat, he patrolled the decks in the bleak evening air, as the vessel slipped down-river toward the sea.

They dropped anchor at Barking Creek. Long-boats came alongside with provisions, including live poultry and a dozen sheep, which were quartered in accommodations near the mainmast.

Dawn saw the *James Gilbert* out in the English Channel, heading west. With a tailwind, good weather, and calm seas, it made excellent time sailing down the coast of Africa. The ship rounded the Cape of Good Hope and veered northeast on the last lap to Bombay.

Six days later, the barometer fell with alarming speed, and within a few hours, the wind had reached gale force. Waves were crashing over the decks. Cabins were flooded, and passengers huddled in the crew's quarters.

A wall of water smashed into the galley, reducing it to chaos. Sails ripped apart, and ropes chafed until they snapped.

On orders of the captain, bags full of oil were hauled out of the main hatch and punctured so that their contents would smooth the water. But the waves were too violent for the oil to have much effect.

For forty-eight hours Captain Carter never left the wheelhouse.

Two men, and sometimes three, were needed to keep the ship on course. Up in the rigging, the sailors risked their lives to shorten the sail that was tearing loose from its lashings.

On the morning of the second day, the storm eased enough to allow the crew to begin clearing up the wreckage.

Then it blew again, although with less ferocity, and Captain Carter went below-decks for a few hours of sleep, leaving the second mate in charge.

In the wheelhouse during the middle watch was the helmsman, assisted by a seaman and an apprentice. The second mate was on the poop deck, supervising a change of sail.

The helmsman, steering the northeasterly course ordered by Captain Carter, was complaining about the quality of the officers aboard when the apprentice nudged his arm. "Pipe down," said the apprentice. "We've got a visitor."

A tall, stocky man in a captain's uniform pushed past the astonished helmsman into the cramped wheelhouse and peered into the compass.

The binnacle light revealed a long and vivid scar running almost the length of the stranger's face. Without looking up, he commanded, "Steer nor' nor'east."

"I'm not taking any orders except the captain's," replied the helmsman indignantly. "He said nor'east."

But the stranger countered angrily, "I said nor' nor'east. And look lively, for every moment counts." Then he opened the door and disappeared onto the deck.

The helmsman didn't know what to do. Should he take the order? The second mate was still out on the deck. Perhaps the man who looked like a captain was a passenger, and was simply transmitting an order from Captain Carter. Satisfied with this explanation, the helmsman spun the wheel. The ship swung slowly into a fresh course.

Captain Carter woke in the early dawn to excited shouting from the deck. He found his crew hurling out ropes to the occupants of four battered lifeboats tossing in the heavy swell on the port side of the *James Gilbert*.

The lifeboats were secured, and more than seventy men in an advanced state of exhaustion and shock clambered up the sides of the great sailing ship.

"We're from the brig *Firebird*, sir," one of the ravaged men explained. "The ship caught fire two days ago. She burned down to the waterline, and then went down. You showed up just in time—we couldn't have lasted another hour."

"Is your captain here?" asked Captain Carter.

"No, sir," the sailor replied. "He was killed as we lowered our boats. The mainmast came down and struck him a fatal blow across the head. He was our only fatality."

The survivors went below for food and medical treatment, and the ship continued on its original course. One hour later, a lookout sighted an odd object bobbing in the water off the starboard bow.

It was the body of a man, a broad-shouldered man with a barrel chest and a vivid scar down the side of his face. And the sleeve of his uniform displayed a captain's rings.

✻ The Haunted Hospital ✻

Hospitals can be scary enough. But what about a haunted hospital? Sydney, Australia's Prince Alfred Hospital has a beautiful ghost nurse who has walked its halls since the mid-1950s.

This anonymous ghostly vision is apparently as dedicated to her job in the afterlife as she was before her tragic and untimely death. She is thought to be the ghost of a once dedicated employee of the hospital who died as a result of a fall from a high verandah. In spite of her injuries, that very night she was back, tending to patients who needed her.

The nurse, called the Good Ghost Sister, has been encountered going into the operating room just before important operations are to be performed. What is she doing there? Checking the instruments? Guiding the hands of the surgeons? Consoling patients? No one seems to know for sure. While her appearance has caused some stress and confusion among the hospital staff, no one seems to fear her seemingly gentle spirit.

In fact, more often than not, this ghostly night sister actually saves lives. More than once she has alerted one of the living on-duty nurses to go to the bedside of a patient right before they are about to experience a life-threatening crisis.

XVII. DO NOT DISTURB!

We often get grumpy when someone wakes us up. When the dead are woken from slumber, they may not be in the best of spirits either, and may take revenge on those who disrupted their peace and quiet. Mummies, giants, witches, and statuary—they all become especially irritated in these next ghost stories.

Revenge of
❖ the Stone Man ❖

Deep in a vault under the 14th-century church in the pretty English village of Cottesbrooke, lay twenty-seven coffins. They had remained undisturbed among the musty cobwebs since the last coffin arrived in 1747.

Then, in 1962, the first shafts of light for more than two hundred years splashed down into the gloom. The vault was opened—and a curse was unleashed upon all who peered down at the musty remains.

There were eight people around the tomb of the Allsop family when it was opened. All of them died within the next four years, some mysteriously, others tragically. And all were said to be the victims of a ghost—Sir Joseph Allsop—the "wicked squire" of Cottesbrooke.

His statue, unsheathed stone sword in hand,

guards his burial place. The legend has it that he could not tolerate anyone tampering with the family vault.

And there had been no tampering—the heavy stone slabs had not been lifted for centuries—until the spring of 1962, when the parish church of St. Michael's underwent restoration. Central heating pipes needed inspection, and this meant entering the vault and moving some flagstones in its wall.

On May 24, watched by the glowering stone figure of Sir Joseph, three workmen pried up the heavy stones that marked the entrance to the vault.

There were onlookers from the parish on the pleasant, warm day, but everyone gathered around the tomb felt a definite chilling of the atmosphere as the stones were lifted. Two of them, the churchwarden's wife, Mrs. Mary Roper, and an elderly woman friend, felt suddenly afraid and left the church. Of all those who witnessed the scene, they are the only two still alive.

"A strange disturbing atmosphere suddenly

surrounded us," Mrs. Roper explained later. "My friend felt it too. We both knew that no good would come of disturbing the sleep of the dead."

The vengeance of Sir Joseph Allsop was not long in making itself felt. The architect who supervised the restoration died suddenly, in early middle age, two weeks later. Three more sudden deaths followed in quick succession—a builder employed on the job, a carpenter, and a surveyor who was supervising the work.

All the deaths were said to be from natural causes. The villagers knew differently.

The church organist, a man in his early thirties, died while halfway through a hymn at an evening service.

A twenty-three-year-old farm worker was found lying unconscious and critically ill in a country lane. His battered bicycle lay nearby. Immediately people asked, "Has he been in the tomb?" It was found that he had. Two days later, he died.

The vault was still open and arrangements were made to have it resealed. Perhaps then the reign of terror would cease and the village could return to sleepy seclusion.

But Sir Joseph, it seemed, was not finished. Near midnight on June 19, an elderly couple walking home along a path near the churchyard heard sounds of violence coming from the church. They hurried to the village and roused the local policeman, but by the time he got to St. Michael's the noise had stopped.

The next morning, clergymen discovered that a dozen coffins had been wrenched from their niches and hurled across the floor like matchsticks in a gale.

The following day, the local grocer died. He was forty-one and often boasted that he had never had a day's illness. Once again, the post mortem showed death to be due to natural causes—this time, heart failure.

The next Sunday, the tomb was sealed and reconsecrated. That, everyone hoped, would be the end of the matter. But it was not.

A spine-chilling and totally inexplicable finale brought the curtain down on the affair—an incident that was to transform an eerie ghost story to a classic tale of the unknown.

Two weeks before Christmas, Reginald Martin,

the elderly sexton of St. Michael's, was found dead in the garden of his home. He was crumpled over his wheelbarrow near a compost heap. He had not been a robust man and it was assumed that the exertion of gardening had been too much for him.

Only two things, two *small* things, dashed the theory to pieces. Martin was the last survivor of the eight who had witnessed the opening of the tomb. And in his hand he grasped a tiny piece of stone.

It was an ordinary piece of stone—*but one that fit exactly into a scar on the end of the sword that the statue of Sir Joseph Allsop held in its hand.*

Leave This Stone
✤ Unturned ✤

All day long the convoys of military trucks groaned through England's east coast villages on their way to the sea. It was early in June 1944, and the Allies were massing on the Channel shores ready to make the perilous journey into France. The D-Day landings were about to begin.

The long line of American tank-carriers that had rumbled for two nights and a day eastbound from their depot pulled up abruptly and unwillingly at the Green in the center of the sleepy village of Great Leighs.

A huge weathered stone, eight feet high and over two tons in weight, stood by the roadside, barring the way of the wide trucks. Schedules were brutally tight. The past had to stand aside while current history was made. A wire hawser lassoed the stone, and it was wrenched from its socket and dragged away.

The convoy moved on. And the village remained—to be tyrannized by the specter whose tombstone had been displaced. For the Witch of Great Leighs's reign of terror has, by its unique and eerie violence, been added to the annals of psychical folklore.

Three hundred years earlier, so the story went, the witch had been buried, with a stake through

her heart, at the Great Leighs crossroads. And she had lain quietly until only a few hours after the stone's removal, when extraordinary things began to happen.

The bell in the church tower tolled in the early hours of the morning—when nobody was near it!

The following Sunday, the bells played reverse chimes—which stopped as soon as anyone entered the church! And for several days running, the church clock struck midnight—at 2:30 in the morning!

A local farmer's haystacks were pushed over during the night, stacks of corn from one meadow were found the next morning in another. Hens stopped laying and chickens were found drowned in water barrels.

Sheep turned up in the wrong field—though their own field was securely gated and the hedges unbroken. Three geese owned by the landlord of a local pub disappeared from his garden overnight and were never seen again.

In a builder's yard, a neatly stacked pile of scaffold poles was found scattered all over. But no noise had been heard during the night.

Practically every adult in the village had a story to tell of unexplained happenings. Within a few days the village was in a state bordering on mass hysteria.

The newspapers sent reporters to investigate. Psychic experts were called in. And still the witch's ghost continued to disrupt the community.

Thirty sheep and two horses were found dead one morning.

Chickens in a yard and rabbits in a hutch mysteriously changed places, yet the fasteners on the hutch had been undisturbed.

A boulder weighing two-hundred pounds was found outside the front door of a pub. Where it had come from no one knew.

In St. Anne's Castle Inn, a bedroom became haunted. The landlord, Arthur Sykes, had placed furniture carefully and tidily about the room, but next morning it was a shambles—a chest of drawers was on its side, bedclothes were strewn over the floor, a wardrobe was in a different position!

Mr. Sykes tidied the room. Next morning it

was a shambles again. He tidied it once more—and the same thing happened.

"I don't understand it," he said. "From the way the room was upset I should certainly have heard something happening, because I was sleeping in the next bedroom. But I heard nothing."

"There is no doubt that the village was subjected to a reign of terror," another reputable man related. "Most of what happened can't possibly be explained naturally.

"In broad daylight I saw a man's straight razor, opened, lying on the street. I went to pick it up and it jumped away from me.

"I tried again and the same thing happened. But it can't have been someone pulling it with a thin thread for a laugh, because it kept jumping *up and down*—it jumped about a foot into the air. Frankly, I was frightened. I left it there in case it attacked me."

It was high time, decided the villagers, that something was done.

A week after the disturbances started, a group of men and women from the town recovered the witch's tombstone from where the soldiers had left it. They dragged it with a tractor, and in a midnight ceremony, replaced it at the crossroads, exactly where it had been for generations.

The hauntings stopped from that moment. Great Leighs has been a peaceful village ever since. The town's witch, it seems, is happy to be home.

Cave of the
❧ August Moon ❧

The Dutch innkeeper and explorer Henry Van Hoevenberg was so famous that Mt. Van Hoevenberg, New York, was named in his honor.

Many fabulous tales were told about Van Hoevenberg. Some of these adventures could have happened, though it's hard to believe the following ever did.

As the story goes, Henry was hiking in his beloved woods when he came across an old parchment map inscribed with the characters of an unknown language. The complicated writing and drawing on the map was faint and blurred. But, nevertheless, Harry insisted that the map gave directions to a vast buried treasure.

The treasure was supposed to be hidden in a cave partway up Mt. Colden, but the cave entrance could only be seen from Mt. McIntyre, when the August moon was at its fullest.

This information frustrated Henry because it was already September when he found the map, and he would have to wait a year to investigate further. But wait he did.

The night of the full moon the following August found him more than five thousand feet up the rugged slope of Mt. McIntyre, as he scanned Mt. Colden for any signs of a cave entrance.

There it was, a dark opening just above a precipice.

Henry, so the story goes, scrambled down McIntyre and up Colden. He found the cave, paused to catch his breath, and then, lighting a small birch-bark torch, he peered into the vault—and entered.

A few yards from the entrance, he spotted several old leather trunks, their handles and sides split and cracked with age. From the broken sides, a trickle of gold coins had fallen to the cave's rock floor.

The explorer was beginning to fill his pockets when he heard a sound behind him, coming from deep within the cave. Suddenly a hideous, transparent, nine-foot-tall man was bearing down on him with a gleaming knife raised high above his head.

Henry dropped the coins and reached for the torch. But before he could retrieve it, the giant was upon him, and the fight began. The torch was stomped out as the man and apparition struggled furiously in the dark.

Although Henry was short, he was strong, and

he fought fiercely. Soon, however, he was shoved over the edge of the cliff into the void below. He remembered his fall being broken by a small tree, and then he remembered crashing onto the ground.

Later he crawled to the shore of Heart Lake, where he was found by searchers. He had two broken legs, three broken ribs, and a broken arm—but also, we are told, glittering gold coins in his pockets to prove his story.

Disbelievers taunted Henry and tried to goad him into returning to the cave. The adventurer stiffly refused. He maintained that he had found the cave's ferocious inhabitant far too unpleasant and unsociable.

❧ The Mummy's Curse ❧

The Princess of Amen-Ra lived some 1,500 years before the birth of Christ. When she died, she was placed in an ornate wooden coffin and buried deep in a vault at Luxor, on the banks of the Nile.

Had she been left undisturbed in her vault, perhaps this would have been the end of the story. In fact, it was only the beginning. For ten years at the start of the 20th century, the evil influence of her coffin brought death and havoc wherever it went.

Of all tales of the supernatural this one is perhaps the best documented, the most disturbing, and the most difficult to explain.

In the late 1890s, four rich young Englishmen visiting the excavations at Luxor were invited to buy an exquisitely fashioned mummy case containing the remains of the Princess of Amen-Ra.

They drew lots. The winner paid several

hundred pounds and had the coffin taken to his hotel. A few hours later he was seen walking out toward the desert. He was never seen again.

The next day, one of his companions was shot by an Egyptian servant. The wound was so severe that his arm had to be amputated.

The third man in the party found on his return home that the bank holding his entire savings had failed.

The fourth man suffered a severe illness, lost his job, and was reduced to selling matches in the street.

Eventually, the coffin reached England, where it was bought by a London businessman. After three members of his family had been injured in a road accident, and his house severely damaged by fire, the owner of the coffin donated it to the British Museum.

Despite its reputation, the authorities agreed to accept the gift. But the Princess of Amen-Ra was not long in bringing calamity to her new home. As the coffin was being unloaded from a truck in the museum courtyard, the truck suddenly went into reverse, trapping a passerby, who was taken to a hospital.

Then, as the casket was being lifted up the stairs by two workmen, one fell and broke his leg. The other man, in his thirties and apparently in perfect health, died unaccountably two days later.

Once the Princess was installed in the Egyptian Room, the trouble really started. Night watchmen at the museum frequently heard frantic hammering and sobbing coming from the coffin.

Other exhibits in the room were hurled about. On one occasion a keeper claimed that he had been attacked by a spirit who leaped out of the casket and tried to hurl him down a delivery chute with a forty-foot drop.

Cleaning personnel at the museum refused to go near the Princess of Amen-Ra after one man derisively flicked a dustcloth at the face painted on the coffin and his child died of measles soon afterward.

Finally, the museum authorities had the mummy moved to the basement, where it could surely do no further harm. Within a week, one of the moving men was seriously ill, and the supervisor of the move was found dead at his desk.

By now the papers had seized the story. A staff photographer took a picture of the mummy case and found when he developed it that the painting on the coffin had changed into a human—and horrifying—face. The photographer went home, locked his door, and shot himself.

The museum then sold the mummy to a private collector. After continual misfortune, he banished it to the attic, where it was languishing when Madame Helena Blavatsky, a well-known authority on the occult, visited the house. She did not know the history of the mummy, or that it was even on the premises. Yet as soon as she entered the house, she was seized with a fit of shivering and declared there was an evil influence of incredible intensity at work.

The host, almost jokingly, invited her to have a look around. Madame Blavatsky searched the house without success, until she came to the attic and found the mummy case. She knew at once that this was the source of the evil influence she had felt.

"Would you be able to exorcise this evil spirit?" asked the host.

"There is no such thing as exorcism in this case," replied Madame Blavatsky. "Evil remains evil forever. Nothing can be done about it. I implore you to rid yourself of this evil thing as soon as possible."

The owner of the house did not take the matter seriously until a week or so later, when a member of his family, moving some suitcases in the attic, claimed to have seen a figure rise from the mummy case and glide across the floor. After this, he decided to take Madame Blavatsky's advice and get rid of the disturbing object.

No British museum would take the mummy; the fact that nearly 20 people had met with death or disaster from handling the casket was now well known.

Eventually, an unsuperstitious, hard-headed American archaeologist who dismissed the happenings as quirks of circumstance paid a very handsome price for the specimen. He then made arrangements for its removal to New York. In April 1912, the collector escorted his prize aboard a sparkling new White Star liner about to make its maiden voyage to New York.

On the night of April 14, amid scenes of unprecedented horror, the Princess Amen-Ra accompanied 1,500 passengers to their deaths at the bottom of the Atlantic. The name of the ship was the *Titanic*.

INDEX

348

If you liked this book, you'll love all the titles in this series:

- Little Giant Book of After School Fun
- Little Giant Book of Amazing Mazes
- Little Giant Book of Brain Twisters
- Little Giant Book of Card Tricks
- Little Giant Book of Dinosaurs
- Little Giant Book of Jokes
- Little Giant Book of Kids' Games
- Little Giant Book of Knock-Knocks
- Little Giant Book of Math Puzzles
- Little Giant Book of Magic Tricks
- Little Giant Book of Optical Illusions
- Little Giant Book of Optical Tricks
- Little Giant Book of Riddles
- Little Giant Book of School Jokes
- Little Giant Book of Science Experiments
- Little Giant Book of Tongue Twisters
- Little Giant Book of Travel Fun
- Little Giant Book of "True" Ghost Stories
- Little Giant Book of Visual Tricks
- Little Giant Book of Whodunits

Available at fine stores everywhere.